喚醒你的英文語感！

Get a Feel for English !

喚醒你的英文語感！

Get a Feel for English !

外商・百大
英文面試

100 Essential Job Interview
Questions and Answers

勝經

作 者◎薛詠文

You're
hired

很榮幸我能替 Wendy 老師的書作個引介。Wendy 老師非常成功地幫助讀者把重點放在有效面試技巧的基本功上。她的建議務實又有用，而收錄在本書中的範例都是相當具指標性的面試問題。這本書的結構條理清晰，能讓你準確地找到所需。

每道面試提問皆有二種答案：第一種回覆是用簡單的英文；第二種是以比較複雜的語言呈現。這點非常實用，因為如此一來，你可以選擇較適合自己英語能力的回覆方式。

Wendy 還為每個問題收錄一串非常實用的字彙，讓你在面對每個問題時，能夠有強而有力的字彙可用。這點一定會使面試官的印象深刻。當你在學習與記憶字彙時，一定要記得看看這些字彙在範例擬答中是如何被使用的。
除了 Wendy 老師高明的建議之外，本人想提供一些自己的意見。

首先是關於履歷表與求職信方面的問題。在面試之前你有可能會以電子郵件的方式將履歷文件傳給求職公司，但是為了面試官的方便，前往面試時你應該帶一份所有履歷文件的副本。記得使用高品質的紙張列印。如果你希望你的文件能從其他求職者的文件當中脫穎而出，能顯現出你的求職企圖與眾不同，就得使用非常高品質的紙，這麼做表示你對自己以及你的成就有充分的自信。

我認為一場成功的面試表現秘訣在於準備。盡你所能找出關於求職公司的一切資訊。可以利用網路找出關於這家公司的最新消息，例如：新聞稿或媒體報導等。如果你能找得到這些資訊的英文版，將會很有幫助，因為這樣

一來，你就可以利用英文的新聞稿蒐集與這家公司、這個產業以及這家公司運作市場相關的字彙。

記得要練習一下你決定在面試中使用之字彙的發音。這麼做可以讓你更有信心，並克服緊張的情緒。

面試時你會有機會提出自己想問的問題，而這麼做是很必要的。有些台灣人對這點感到害羞，因為他們認為在面試中問問題是不禮貌的。但是請記得，面試官也會依據你對公司的提問來評斷你。盡量避免提出關於工作以及工作條件的問題；相反地，可以詢問關於這家公司目前正面臨的問題，這表示你了解公司的狀況並且很感興趣。

再一則建議則是關於你的外表。留下良好的第一印象很重要，而這意味你必須看起來端莊。如果你是男士，應穿著正式的西裝、打領帶，並記得把你的鞋子擦亮！如果妳是女士，則應穿戴素淨的首飾，但是不要化太濃的妝。

最後再次強調，按照 Wendy 老師於書中提供的絕佳建議去做，相信你一定會有很好的機會得到你真正想要的工作。

Quentin Brand

（本文作者為貝塔語言「愈忙愈要學英文」系列暢銷叢書作者，現為登峰美語名師）

It is my great pleasure to introduce this book by Wendy Hsueh. She has done an excellent job in helping readers to focus on the basics of good interview technique. Her suggestions are practical and useful, and the sample questions she has included in the book are pretty standard for most interviews. The book is clearly and easily organized so you can find exactly what you are looking for.

Each question has two answers—the first in easy English, and the second in more complex language. This is really useful as it allows you to choose a response more suitable to your English ability.

Wendy has also included a very useful vocabulary list for each question, giving you power words to use in response to each question. This will surely impress the interviewer. When you are building your vocabulary, be sure to look at how the vocabulary is used in the example answers.

In addition to Wendy's excellent advice, I'd like to offer my own.

First, regarding your CV and cover letter. You will probably send them electronically to the company before the interview. But you should bring a copy of all your documents to the interview for the convenience of the interviewer. Use high quality paper to print this. You want your documents to stand out from other candidates, to show that your application is different from others, so use very high quality paper. This will show that you have pride in your self and your achievements.

I think the secret to a good interview performance is in the preparation. Try to find out as much as you can about the company. Use the internet to find out the latest information from the company, for example: press-releases, media reports, and so on. If you can try to find this information in English, this will be helpful. You can use the English press-releases to collect vocabulary about the company, the industry and the market the company operates in.

Remember to practice the pronunciation of the vocabulary you decide to use in the interview. This will help you to be more confident and to deal with your nerves.

In the interview you will have the chance to ask your own questions. It is essential that you do this. Some Taiwanese are shy about this, because they think it's not polite to ask questions in an interview. But remember, the interviewer will also judge you on the questions you ask about the company. Try to avoid questions about the job, and about the terms and conditions of the job. Instead, ask questions about current issues the company is facing. This will show that you are knowledgeable about the company's situation and interested in it.

One more piece of advice is your appearance. It's important to make a good first impression, and this means looking good. If you are a guy, wear a formal suit and tie, and remember to polish your shoes! If you are a woman, wear quiet jewellery, and don't wear too much make up.

Once again, follow Wendy's excellent advice in the book, and I'm sure you will have an good chance of getting the job you really want.

Quentin Brand

在現今競爭異常激烈的就業市場上，想要略勝他人一籌的關鍵是什麼？考試分數？成績排名？得獎經驗？還是證照張數多寡？這些不能說完全不重要，但是在這個已然是地球村的就業市場上，致勝的首要關鍵是要有『國際觀』。

台灣已是一個邁入國際化的社會，國內有很多的外商或大企業的求職面談皆需使用英文進行；另外，若是想去其他國家求職（比方說美國、澳洲或新加坡等），英文更是面談時會使用的第一語言。為了滿足求職面談和英文表達這兩大需求，並幫助讀者前進國際職場，筆者因而有了《外商·百大英文面試勝經》一書的構想。希望本書的誕生可以協助讀者在求職路上和英語表達方面有所助益。的確，若能排除語言的障礙，在國際職場您就能秀出自己的專長和優勢，讓自己真正地『被看見』！

本書包括三大部分，分別是「你一定要知道的面試策略」、「英文面試一定要會回答的 100 個問題」、「面試好用字彙補給」，附錄則是為爭取面試機會的「求職書信準備範例」，其中第二部分面談最常被問到的 100 個問題與參考擬答是本書的重點。這 100 個問題可說是筆者在外商資訊產業工作近十五年的親身經驗，或自己曾經聽聞蒐集到的問題集。書中除針對每個問題提供「面試一點通」及「有力簡答」和「深入詳答」兩種擬答之外，同時還提供「必通實用句型」及「面試好用字彙」，希望可以協助應試者在準備面談的同時，也能增進自身英語程度與重要字彙的運用能力。

在此要特別強調，讀者雖然身處台灣，但眼光要放大、放遠，必須培養出能和世界接軌的國際觀。因此，在準備面談題目與回答時，無須分別這是

「外商會問的問題」或這是「台灣公司會問的問題」，須知面談時的發問權主要是掌握在面試官手上，他或她會問什麼問題，不可能事先透露或可精準預測。本書以不同的角度出發，將外商企業面談時的多樣化問題仔細歸納整理，盡量涵蓋外商雇主可能提及的問題，讓應試者先有概念並預想答案，思考如何呈現自己的長處和優勢，最大化並有效地推銷自己。

當然，每個人都有自己不同的專長和希望投身的工作領域，在參考本書各個問題所提供的最佳擬答之後，務必再針對自己的專業領域設想適合自己情況和條件的答案。因此每道問題後的 "My own answer" 空白處，就是留給您草擬自己可能的回答。

熟悉了英語面談的問答架構之後，再搭配逐步培養出的英語能力，這對應試者而言將會是如虎添翼，肯定可以提高錄取的機會。當然，準備英語面談不僅僅只是為了得到一份工作就了事，更進一步的深層意義是，讀者可藉由揣摩問題和答案建立起一個屬於自己「具邏輯性」的思考模式。這樣的思考模式在往後進入職場後的溝通將會有莫大的助益。

薛詠文

CONTENTS 目錄

Section 1　你一定要知道的面試策略

Section 2　英文面試一定要會回答的 100 個問題

Part 4 關於未來工作的問題：發展／期望

Part 6 應徵者適合提出的問題與結束感謝用語

☑ 應徵者適合提出的問題

Section 3 ▶ 面試好用詞彙補給

附錄 ▶ 履歷表、求職信及後續追蹤信件範例

1. 履歷表 (Curriculum Vitae)

2. 求職信 (Cover Letter)

3. 後續追蹤信件 (Follow-up Letter)

📖 本書使用說明

本書主要學習內容為 Section 2〈面試一定要會回答的 100 個問題〉，每道題目規劃為跨頁呈現的獨立單元，左頁為「關鍵問題」、「最佳擬答」，右頁則收錄了「Tips 面試一點通」、「必通實用句型」及「好用字彙」，並預留了讓讀者擬答的空間。

面試問題

共有 100 道英文面試常見問題。

MP3 編號

MP3 的音軌編號，各單元以「提問問題→有力簡答→深入詳答」順序錄製。

有力簡答

針對面試問題所做的簡短擬答，針對重點作說明，文句精簡有力，若面談時間有限或是參加聯合面試，可多練習熟記這類有力簡答，臨場更能靈活套用、應對。

深入詳答

針對面試問題所作的深入擬答，除了回答重點，也會以不同行業或職務內容為例，進一步舉出相關實例或完整的情境說明，讓主考官有更深入的了解。

Q 37

What was the biggest accomplishment in your last position?
你上一個工作最大的成就為何？

A1 有力簡答 （以提升業績為例） Track 38

I was sent to our branch office in Sigapore and helped them to win back major clients and boost the company's revenue by 25%.

我被派到新加坡的分公司去，協助他們贏回主要的大客戶，並大幅增加了公司的營收達 25%。

A2 深入詳答

The most satisfying accomplishment I had was that I was assigned to one of our branch offices in Sigapore that was notorious for not growing their sales revenue. The branch lost around six big enterprise clients in a seven-month period prior to my arrival. I worked closely with local clients, constructed proper network structures based on their needs, and successfully implemented cases for enterprise clients. Thus the branch regained its good reputation and sales revenue increased by approximately 25%.

我最令人滿意的成就就是，有次我被指派到新加坡的分公司，那裡因為營收無法成長而為大家所詬病。在我過去之前，分公司在七個月內失去了大約六個大企業客戶。我跟當地的客戶密切地合作，根據他們的需求建構了適合他們的網路架構，並成功地為企業客戶執行了幾個案子。分公司因此重獲好名聲，營收也增加了大約 25%。

90

TIPS 面試一點通

針對每道問題提供回答技巧指引，包括答題時應強調的重點或應避免提及的事項。

Tips 面試一點通！

這是所有產業老闆必問的問題。回答時可照實將自己做得好的部分精簡描述出來，但需注意要以明確的方式來表達。比方說，若只回答「我業績做得很好」，會讓人無法理解「很好是多好？」；若是能具體說出類似「我協助公司提升了 10% 的業績。」這樣明確的陳述，聽者就能有較清楚的概念。

必通實用句型

從最佳擬答選出方便靈活套用的好用句型，可依自身工作條件或狀況修改使用。

Useful Expression 必通實用句型

I helped [company] regained good reputation and boost company's revenue by [amount].
我協助〔公司〕重獲好名聲，大幅增加了公司的營收達〔數字〕。

Power Vocabulary 好用字彙

好用字彙

精選最佳擬答中出現的面試重點字彙，在回答相關面試問題時也可靈活運用。

branch office 分公司
boost [bust] (v.) 提高；增加
satisfying [ˋsætɪsˏfaɪɪŋ] (adj.) 令人滿意的
assign [əˋsaɪn] (v.) 指派
enterprise [ˋɛntəˏpraɪz] (n.) 企業
arrival [əˋvaɪvl] (n.) 到來
implement [ˋɪmpləmənt] (v.) 執行
reputation [ˏrɛpjəˋteʃən] (n.) 名聲

win back 重獲
revenue [ˋrɛvəˏnju] (n.) 收入；收益
accomplishment [əˋkɑmplɪʃmənt] (n.) 成就
notorious [noˋtorɪəs] (adj.) 惡名昭彰的
prior to 在……之前
construct [kənˋstrʌkt] (v.) 建構
regain [rɪˋgen] (v.) 重獲
approximately [əˋprɑksəmɪtlɪ] (adv.) 大約

My own answer

My Own Answer

請針對此題寫下自己的回答，可運用上方的必通句型、字彙，或是 Section 3〈面試好用字彙補給〉，統整自己的最佳擬答，方便面談前隨時查用複習。

Section 1

你一定要知道的
面試策略

- 雇主最在意的事
- 面試前的準備功課
- 面試時該做與不該做的事

雇主最在意的事

　　筆者在資訊產業界工作近十五年期間，參與過無數面談會議。每當老闆問及申請者「你為什麼有興趣來我們公司上班？」這類問題時，所得到的回答（尤其是初入社會的新鮮人）都是偏向「**以個人角度出發，一味為自己著想**」的答案。比方說，「因為我上個月剛退伍（或畢業），我父親叫我馬上去找份工作……」、「因為我對行銷很有興趣，剛好貴公司正在找人……」，或是「因為我要付房租，還有一個小孩要養，所以想找個薪水較高的工作……」等這類答案。筆者雖然不會讀心術，但是從老闆的表情看來，不難猜出老闆聽到這類答案時心裏可能會反問：「你剛退伍，所以我就有義務要收留你嗎？」、「你對行銷有興趣，所以我就有責任開公司讓你嘗試嗎？」，或是想大聲說「你需要高薪才想來上班，我們公司又不是開慈善機構的！」的確，很多時候，作老闆的是這樣想的。

　　這聽起來既現實又殘酷，但是套句房地產大亨唐納川普 (Donald Trump) 所說的：**"It's nothing personal, it's all about business."**。商業界本來就是這樣，我們要知道，老闆辛辛苦苦地經營一家公司，目的就是要「**賺錢**」並「**永續經營**」，所以才會需要招聘「能夠幫公司賺錢」和「能規劃長遠策略」的優秀人才進公司來協助他。老闆經營公司的目的絕對不是為了某個人的私人需求。企業老闆和應徵者亦非親非故，不論應徵者對什麼有興趣，若與協助公司獲利無關，老闆根本也不會在意。

　　因此，應徵者在準備面談問答之前，一定要有一個正確的觀念，那就是「不可從個人角度出發」來回答問題，而必須「將自己放在老闆的位置，設身處地為老闆與公司著想」。如此換個角度，所說出來的話也會跟著有所不同。請比較以下兩個例子：

例1 （以個人角度出發）

應徵者 A　我想到貴公司上班，因為聽說公司的薪水和福利很好……

老　　闆　我們公司可不是開慈善事業的……

例 2 （設身為求職公司著想）

應徵者 B 我所學的課程和經驗都與貴公司的產品和銷售模式相關，我有信心可幫貴公司提升業績……

老　　闆 喔？你有什麼可以協助銷售的好方法？說來聽聽……

看出差異了嗎？**面談要成功，絕對不能只想到自己的需求。**記得，面談時花錢請人的公司老闆才是主角。**應試者應該將老闆的需求看得比自己個人的需求更重要，才會贏得對方的賞識，在眾多面試者裡脫穎而出。**那麼，企業雇主的需求可能會是什麼呢？ 在面談中雇主所在意的事或想得到的答案又會是哪些呢？

以下十件事，是雇主最在意的事，且會據以判斷應徵者是否為最佳人選的關鍵：

① **Can this person work well with others?**
此人是否能與他人共事？

② **Is the person a leader or a follower?**
此人是領導人才還是部屬人才？

③ **How does the person relate with colleagues?**
此人如何與同事建立關係？

④ **Is the person a team player?**
此人是否可以跟團隊成員合作無間？

⑤ **How can this person contribute to the company?**
此人能否為公司帶來貢獻？

⑥ **Is this person truly qualified for the position?**
此人真的可以勝任此職務嗎？

⑦ **Is this person realistic in terms of abilities and goals?**
此人的能力和目標是否切合實際狀況？

⑧ **Is this person trainable in the tasks and ways of our company?**

針對工作內容和公司目標，此人是否有可塑性？

⑨ **Does this person have the motivation to work hard and do well?**

此人是否有全力以赴的動機？

⑩ **Why does this person want to work for our company?**

此人為什麼會想在本公司工作？

請把這十個要點記在心中，在面談中回答老闆問題時，就比較不會一直往「個人需求」的方向去，而比較能貼近老闆的立場與想法，提出對這個職位、部門和全公司有利且有意義的內容。

面試前的準備功課

筆者十年前在美國的一家書店看過一本有關求職教戰的書，書名叫做《不要寄出履歷表》（*Don't send a CV*）。當時有點納悶：找工作的第一步不就是要準備好制式的履歷表，然後大量撒出，再等有興趣的公司回覆嗎？這本書怎麼會教人不要將履歷表寄出去呢？在仔細地閱讀了之後，才了解貫穿全書的精神要旨，原來是要教人：**先別急著亂撒履歷表，而是應該先針對要去面談的公司、職缺及其工作內容做徹底研究，在用心撰寫一份符合那家公司及那個職缺所需的求職信與履歷表之後，再將它們寄出。**

的確，求職的第一步，在撰寫履歷表和準備面談問題之前，應該先做的事就是將求職的目標公司、產品、客戶群、職位、工作內容及徵求人才條件等細節資訊做一番徹底研究。如此一來，在面談時才能夠針對該公司和產品提出深入的見解。相反地，要是面談時老闆提出一些相關問題，求職者一問三不知，或僅能說說表面空泛的答案，是很難引起老闆共鳴的，也不可能在眾多競爭的求職者中脫穎而出，得到老闆的賞識。

在徹底了解了求職公司的需求之後，接著就是要好好調整自己的心態

了。如同先前提過的，求職者不可抱著「我是為了某某原因而找工作的……」這種心態，而必須自問：「我進入這家公司可以為公司創造出什麼成績？」。已故的蘋果公司（Apple）創辦人及執行長賈伯斯（Steve Jobs）曾說過："We've got to find what we love."（我們必須找到我們之所愛。）的確，**求職者一定要對某個領域有特別的熱情，才有辦法在那個領域展現才能。切記，一定要想清楚自己的興趣為何、有什麼不可取代的能力，和自己要的是什麼**，也就是應先找到自己真正想發展且充滿熱情的領域，如此一來，在面談時才能夠讓老闆感受到你的雄心與積極度，進而爭取到為公司服務的機會。

　　最後，筆者在下方列出準備面談時需額外注意的事項確認清單，供讀者在面談前參考。

☑ 面試前 **3-4** 天的準備：

☐ **事前練習**：找親人或朋友當聽眾或自己對著鏡子，將所準備的答案演練數次，直到熟悉為止。
☐ **職缺資訊**：將求職公司與工作職缺的相關資訊記錄下來或列印出來，以便面試當天隨時參考。
☐ **睡眠充足**：面談前一晚不可熬夜，一定要有充分的睡眠，以確保面談當日頭腦清楚。
☐ **交通動線**：事先查好面談公司的位置、如何前往，以及需預留的交通時間等資訊。

☑ 面試當天的準備：

☐ **文件齊備**：確定履歷表、求職信、推薦信、畢業證書、成績單、證照等文件皆帶齊。
☐ **妝扮得宜**：服裝以商務套裝最佳，髮妝以自然舒適為宜。配件（皮鞋、包包、記事本等）可選用質感較佳的單品，可自然流露出個人品味。
☐ **自信滿滿**：請以自然的笑容與從容不迫的態度，搭配自信心與積極進取的精神應試。

面試時該做與不該做的事

終於獲得申請公司通知面試了，赴約前請務必先了解下列面試前的提醒，哪些事情該留意，哪些部分又該盡量避免，才能讓你在最後一關完美演出，獲得面試官青睞，得到心目中的理想職缺！

Do's 面試時 應做的事	1. 事前準備：面談前先將公司、產品、職缺工作內容都研究清楚。（這些資訊可自求職公司官網上取得。）另外，將交通路線、時間、所需文件、證書、服裝配件等備妥。穿著正式套裝為佳，並提早五至十分鐘到達。
	2. 第一印象：從踏進公司跟接待人員談話開始，就要保持笑容、注意禮貌，聲音語調須和緩從容。
	3. 保持自信：態度自若，和老闆初次會面握手時應穩定有力。眼神保持篤定，說話時適當地和老闆保持眼神的接觸。
	4. 展現熱忱：言談之間自然流露出對該公司或工作的高度興趣，展現願意與團隊合作以達成工作目標的意願。
	5. 強調優點：面談可是自我推銷的一個過程，既然要推銷自己，就必須要強調自己的優點，凸顯個人跟他人不同的特出之處。
	6. 據實回答：雖然凸顯個人特質是必要的，但是不可過於誇大。應針對問題據實回答，不要扭曲或加油添醋。
	7. 積極正面：在面談中有可能討論到個人的弱點，記得要保持積極正面的態度，展現決心並有提出具體修正方案。
	8. 聰明提問：面談最後若有讓求職者提問的機會時，要盡可能提出與工作相關且具有意義的問題。記得，這也是老闆測驗求職者臨場反應和思考邏輯的機會。

Don'ts 面試應 避免的事	1. 消極負面：切忌凡事都往壞處想，不論什麼問題都先預設立場，認為一切都困難重重、無法辦到。老闆是不會欣賞這種消極的人。
	2. 飲食咀嚼：面談時吃東西、喝飲料、嚼口香糖等是絕對禁止的。若是午、晚餐形式的面談會議，口中有食物時則應避免說話。
	3. 簡答含糊：回答問題時僅以 "Yes"、"No" 或 "Maybe" 等字詞帶過，卻不給明確的答案。這無形中會顯示出求職者語言表達能力有問題。
	4. 誇大其詞：不論回答什麼問題都加油添醋，將之前做過的成績加以誇大、虛報。小心在產業界待久了的老闆可是能輕易聽得出其中破綻的。
	5. 語氣微弱：表達時氣若游絲，聲音微小，讓老闆聽得極為吃力。這顯示出求職者自信不足。
	6. 聲響干擾：手機、電子錶沒有關機，導致面談中鈴聲大作，干擾到談話。這顯示出求職者對自我要求不高，自我控制能力不足。
	7. 口無遮攔：言談中講到與工作無關的私事或家庭紛爭等，都是不必要的。也不要自做聰明地想講笑話來顯示幽默感。
	8. 文不對題：主考官問 A，求職者卻答 B。這顯示出求職者抓不到問題要點，恐怕將來在工作上也無法勝任。

NOTES

Section 2

英文面試一定要
會回答的 100 個問題

Part 1

開場寒喧用語──關鍵 90 秒

The Most Important 90 Seconds

經過一連串的文件準備、蒐集求職公司相關資訊和事前反覆地自我演練後，終於來到面試當天，求職者自信滿滿地到達公司進行面試。人和人在不認識的狀況之下，第一印象除了由「表象因素」（包括外貌、穿著、髮型及化妝等）來判斷之外，更重要的就是由初步的「個人談吐」和「溝通能力」來判定了。面談者藉由幾個簡單的寒暄對話，就可判斷出應徵者對狀況的掌控能力。請先參考以下的錯誤示範：

Interviewer: How are you doing today, Ms. Chang?
（面試官：張小姐，妳今天好嗎？）

Ms. Chang: Well, not like I want to mention it, but my dog is sick, so it's been kind of a bad day for me.
（張小姐：嗯，不是我想提起，可是因為我的狗生病了，所以我今天不太好過。）

由以上的例子可看出，求職者似乎搞不清楚狀況。面試官所問的 "How are you doing?" 只是一般的寒暄問候語，不是真的要聽她講一些生活瑣事。那麼，要怎樣回答才能讓面試官認為求職者是對狀況掌控能力佳的人，並因而留下良好的第一印象呢？以下我們來看看面試官可能提出的寒暄語和求職者可能的回答：

 **Track 01**

面試官可能會提的寒暄用語	應徵者可參考的禮貌回應
How are you doing today, Ms. Chang? 張小姐，妳今天好嗎？	I am doing great. Thank you. And yourself? 我很好，謝謝。您呢？
Please take a seat. 請坐。	Thank you. 謝謝。
Thank you for coming all the way from Tao-Yuan. 謝謝妳專程從桃園趕來。	No problem at all. It's my pleasure. I am really looking forward to our discussion today. 沒問題的，這是我的榮幸。我很期待我們今天的討論。

Did you have any difficulty finding our location? 我們的地點好找嗎？有沒遇到什麼困難？	**Not at all, thank you for asking. Your directions were really helpful.** 完全沒問題，謝謝關心。您提供的指引幫助很大。
Would you like something to drink? 妳想喝點什麼嗎？	**Thank you. If it's not any trouble, can I just have a cup of tea please?** 謝謝，如果不麻煩的話，我可以就要杯茶嗎？

一般來說面談的主導者是公司的面試官，因此在不喧賓奪主的情況下應以回答面試官的問題為主。但若求職者真的想主動說些寒暄的句子來增加和面試官的互動，可以參考以下適合談論的主題：

適合主題	應徵者可主動提出的互動用語	可預期的回答
天氣狀況	**Today's weather is really nice, isn't?** 今天天氣真不錯，不是嗎？	**Yeah, it really is.** 是呀，天氣真的。
辦公環境	**You have a very nice office.** 您們的辦公室很不錯。	**Oh, I am glad you think so.** 噢，我很高興妳這麼認為。
交通狀況	**The traffic is really terrible out there. It's a good thing that I took the MRT.** 外面交通狀況很糟。幸好我搭捷運來。	**You are here on time.** 你準時到達。

再次說明，整場面談是以公司的面談主管為主導者，求職者雖可以主動提出些輕鬆的話題來增進互動，但是要應避免沒完沒了地聊下去。記得要將主導權交給面談主管，並以回答他們希望得到的資訊為主。求職者自己提出的寒暄性的對話應點到即止，以利後續面談的進行。

Part 2
關於申請者本身的問題：背景／特質

Questions about the Applicant:
Background / Personal Characteristics

Q1

Tell me more about yourself. /
Please introduce yourself.

請介紹一下自己。

 Track 02

I just graduated from ABC University, and I've obtained my bachelor's degree in business management. Although I don't have much working experience, I do have a passion for my work.

我剛從 ABC 大學畢業，我已取得企管的大學學位。雖然我沒有很多工作經驗，但是對工作充滿熱情。

A2 深入詳答

Sure, no problem. Well, I grew up here in Taipei. After graduating from high school, I was accepted by National ABC University to major in business administration. While at ABC University, I began specializing in working with local market research firms, and I haven't looked back since. I've been working in the market research field for over three years now, developing and implementing strategies that help business clients understand more about market trends and consumer needs. Over the years, I've developed strong analyzing skills, organizational skills, and most importantly a passion for my work.

好的，沒問題。嗯，我在台北長大。高中畢業之後，我便進入國立 ABC 大學主修企業管理。在 ABC 大學期間，我就開始專門與本地行銷研究公司合作，至今從沒改變過我的選擇。我已經在市場研究領域工作超過三年的時間，負責開發和執行可協助企業客戶更了解市場和消費者需求的策略。過去幾年間，我鍛鍊出了優秀的分析能力、組織能力，而最重要的是，我對工作的熱忱。

Tips 面試一點通！

通常面試一開始，面試官常會問這樣的問題來開啟互動，只要簡單、直接地表達自己主要的專才和能力即可，不需太過詳細地介紹唸過的學校或待過公司等瑣碎細節。

Useful Expression 必通實用句型

I've been working in the [type of work] field for over [number] years.

我已經在〔工作型態〕領域超過〔數字〕的時間。

Power Vocabulary 好用字彙

obtain [əb`ten] (v.) 獲得
specialize [`spɛʃəl͵aɪz] (v.) 專門從事；專攻
strategy [`strætədʒɪ] (n.) 策略；計畫
analyzing skill 分析能力
passion [`pæʃən] (n.) 熱忱；熱情

bachelor [`bætʃələ] (n.) 學士（常大寫）
implement [`ɪmpləmənt] (v.) 實施；執行
trend [trɛnd] (n.) 趨勢
organizational skill 組織能力

My own answer

What are your strengths and weaknesses?

你的長處與弱點為何？

A1 有力簡答

I have good communication skills and I am able to speak English fluently. As for my weaknesses, well, I would say sometimes I pay too much attention to details.

我的溝通能力強，也能夠說流利的英語。至於我的缺點，嗯，我覺得有時我太過注重細節了。

A2 深入詳答

I consider my communication skills and language ability my two strengths. This combination enables me to communicate with clients from around the world without any difficulties, and my boss is very complimentary about my work too. As for my weaknesses, well, I have to admit that sometimes I pay too much attention to details. When I am working on a task, I can't help wanting to make sure everything is perfect and I spend lots of time checking over and over again. However, now I've come to a good balance by ensuring all my tasks are done accurately the first time.

我認為我的溝通技巧和語言能力是我的兩大長處。這兩個能力的結合讓我可以毫無阻礙地跟來自世界各地的客戶溝通，而且我老闆也對我的表現讚賞有佳。至於我的弱點，我必須承認我有時候會太注重細節。當我在做事時，我會忍不住想確認所有的事都完美無缺，我會花很多時間一再地檢查。但是，現在我學會了如何取得平衡，我會確認在第一次就把事情做對。

Tips 面試一點通！

一般人都會覺得討論自己的長處或優點是個有點棘手的問題，其實只要把握一個原則——誠實描述即可，絕不可誇大。提到自己的長處或優點時，只提及與工作相關者爲上策。若要討論的是個人的弱點，則有幾個策略：

第一，要將弱點淡化，改以正面的方式來呈現。比方說，若你是個「慢郎中」，可以較正面的方式說「個人比較注重細節，因此完成專案的時間會長一點。」其二，直接說出弱點，但要加強補充個人已採取行動做出的改變。比方說，「個人之前較不善於在眾人面前說話，但是在去年上了一系列簡報、溝通及談判技巧的課程之後，學到很多，現在上台報告已不再是個問題。」

Useful Expression 必通實用句型

I consider my [adjective / noun] skills and [adjective / noun] ability my two strengths. As for my weaknesses, well, I have to admit that sometimes I pay too much attention to [something].
我認為我的〔形容詞／名詞〕技巧和〔形容詞／名詞〕能力是我個人的兩大長處。至於我的弱點，我必須承認我有時候會太注重〔某事〕。

My boss is very complimentary about my work.
我老闆對我的工作讚賞有嘉。

Power Vocabulary 好用字彙

strength [strɛŋθ] (n.) 強項
combination [ˌkɑmbəˋneʃən] (n.) 結合
admit [ədˋmɪt] (v.) 承認
accurately [ˋækjərɪtlɪ] (adv.) 精準地

weakness [wiknɪs] (n.) 弱點
complimentary [ˌkɑmpləˋmɛntərɪ] (adj.) 恭維的
attention [əˋtɛnʃən] (n.) 注意；注意力

✎ My own answer

Q3

What are your strongest skills?

你最擅長的技能是什麼？

 **Track 04**

I would say that my strongest skill is computer database programming. I took programming-related courses in university and I learned to design databases to trace customers' records.

我認為寫電腦資料庫程式是我的強項。在大學時我修過程式相關課程，學到如何設計資料庫來追蹤客戶記錄。

A2 深入詳答

Well, I have strong computer database programming skills. I took programming related courses in college, and I learned how to design and maintain customer databases and now I am good at producing desktop presentations too. When I worked at Core-Data Company, I designed a database that maintained all of the customers' information. From that database, sales people were able to trace transaction records and thus analyze consumers' purchasing behaviors. In addition, I transformed the resulting analysis into a clear presentation file for sales managers to review. So I would say that my database programming skill is my strongest skill.

嗯，我的電腦資料庫程式能力頗強。我在大學時修習過程式相關的課程，學到如何設計和維護客戶的資訊庫，現在，我在做電腦簡報方面也很在行。當我在 Core-Data 公司工作時，我設計了一個維護所有客戶資料的資料庫。業務人員可以藉此資料庫追蹤所有的交易記錄，進而分析消費者的購買行為。此外，我還將分析結果轉換成清楚的簡報檔案，以便讓業務經理檢閱。所以，我自認寫資料庫程式是我最擅長的技能。

Tips 面試一點通！

一個人可能會有很多專長或技能，但是面試時只需精簡地提出自己最為擅長的一項即可，而且一定要與面談的工作有相關性的。

Useful Expression 必通實用句型

I would say that my strongest skill is [something]. I took [subject] related-courses in college, and I learned to do [do something].

我認為〔某事〕是我的強項。我在大學時修過〔科目〕相關課程，我學會如何〔作某事〕。

Power Vocabulary 好用字彙

programming [`progræmɪŋ] (n.) 程式
trace [tres] (v.) 追蹤
behavior [bɪ`hevjə] (n.) 行為

maintain [men`ten] (v.) 維護
transaction [træn`zækʃən] (n.) 交易
transform [træns`fɔrm] (v.) 使改變；改善

My own answer

Q4 >

How do you work under pressure? / How do you handle stress?
你如何在有壓力的環境下工作？／你的抗壓性如何？

A1 有力簡答　（以簡報情境為例）

 Track 05

I usually manage stress well and perform better under pressure, so working in a challenging environment is not a problem for me.

我通常都能做好壓力管理，而且在壓力下反而工作更賣力，因此在有挑戰性的環境下工作對我來說不成問題。

A2 深入詳答

I enjoy working in a challenging environment more than in an easy environment, and as a matter of fact, I personally do perform better under pressure. I manage stress well because I always prepare fully before any important events such as presentations and meetings with key clients. For example, if I am depending on using a projector for an important sales presentation, I always arrange for a back-up projector to be available, or print out paper copies of the PowerPoint slides in case all else fails. I think full preparation helps me counter fears and negative thoughts before and during the event and thus helps me manage stress better.

比起輕鬆的環境，我比較喜歡在有挑戰性的環境下工作。事實上，我個人在壓力下反而會有較好的表現。我壓力控管得很好，因為我在重要的活動，比方說簡報或和大客戶開會前，都會做好萬全準備。比方說，如果我要做一場業務簡報會用到投影機，我就會準備一台備用投影機，或將投影片列印成紙本，以防其他都失靈。我認為有周全的準備可在活動前或活動中幫我戰勝恐懼和負面想法，並讓我可以更有效地掌控壓力。

Tips 面試一點通！

這是面試很典型的問題，老闆想知道應徵者的抗壓性如何、是否有辦法在壓力之下還能有好的表現。回答時不要只說「我抗壓性很高」這類空泛的答案，應該舉出實例來說明。

Useful Expression 必通實用句型

I manage [something] well because I always prepare fully.
我〔某事〕管理得很好，因為我都會在事先做好萬全準備。

Power Vocabulary 好用字彙

challenging [`tʃælɪndʒɪŋ] (*adj.*) 有挑戰性的
pressure [`prɛʃə] (*n.*) 壓力
presentation [ˌprizɛn`teʃən] (*n.*) 簡報
available [ə`veləbl] (*adj.*) 可取得的
negative thoughts 負面消極的想法

perform [pə`fɔrm] (*v.*) 表現；履行
projector [prə`dʒɛktə] (*n.*) 投影機
back-up [`bæk͵ʌp] (*adj.*) 支援的 (*n.*) 支援
counter [`kaʊntə] (*v.*) 抵抗；抵消

✎ **My own answer**

Q5

How many foreign languages can you speak?

你會講幾種外語？

 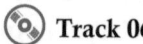

Mandarin Chinese is my mother tongue, and I can also speak English well.

國語是我的母語，另外，我英語也說得不錯。

A2 深入詳答

Besides Mandarin Chinese, I also communicate with my family members and some friends in Taiwanese. I am also pretty proud of my English ability. Not only was I a member of the English debating team in college, but I also scored 900 on the TOEIC exam last month. In order to keep sharpening my English skills I plan to take some more advanced English courses next month.

除了中文之外，我也會跟家人和一些朋友用台語溝通。我也對本身的英文能力感到相當自豪。我不單在大學時是英文辯論隊的一員，上個月我也拿到多益考試 900 分的高分。為了讓自己的英文技巧純熟，我計畫下個月開始去上些更進階的英語課程。

Tips 面試一點通！

在現今國際化的商業環境中，外語能力（尤其是英語）可以說是基本條件需求。被問到此題目時，當然要據實以答，若明明不懂日文，卻硬回答說「會一點」，這樣終究是會破功的。另外，若英語程度尚未純熟，也可以說明已採取哪些行動來加強。

Useful Expression 必通實用句型

I am pretty proud of my [certain ability].

我對自己的〔某項能力〕感到相當自豪。

Power Vocabulary 好用字彙

proud [praud] (*adj.*) 自豪的；驕傲的
score [skor] (*v.*) （考試等中）得分
advanced [əd`vænst] (*adj.*) 進階的

debating team 辯論隊
sharpen [`ʃɑrpn̩] (*v.*) 磨練；使鋒利

✎ **My own answer**

Q6

What is your work style?
你的工作風格為何？

 Track 07

A1 有力簡答

I keep a steady pace on my projects, and ensure that all assigned tasks are done accurately. Also, in order to keep improving, I welcome feedback from my managers and other colleagues.

我在處理案子上採取穩當的步伐，以確保交付的任務都可以正確無誤地完成。另外，為了不斷進步，我也樂於接納主管和同事提供我的意見。

A2 深入詳答

I like doing things step by step. I used to work very quickly and multi-task a lot. However, I then found that if my energy was too spread out on many projects, it was easy to find myself "off balance" and not paying enough attention to important areas of my life, so I got very frustrated and stressed out. I've learned to find a good balance between work and life. I now keep a steady pace on projects and always welcome feedback from other team members. I feel more comfortable working in a cooperative and flexible environment.

我喜歡按部就班地做事。我以前總是動作很快，並同時處理很多事。但是後來我發現如果把精神過度分散在很多案子上，很容易會覺得自己「失去平衡」，同時也無法關注生活中其他重要的層面，因此會陷入強大的挫敗與壓力之中。我已經學會在工作與生活中找到平衡。現在我在處理案子上採取較穩當的步伐，也樂於接受其他同事的意見。我在注重合作並保有彈性的工作環境中更容易發揮。

Tips 面試一點通！

老闆問此問題是想得知應徵者的工作風格是否可和公司文化與行事風格相符。因此，在面談前就應先做足功課，了解該公司的文化、作風等。但在面談時也不要一味地迎合公司，而應該將自己的工作風格誠實以告。

Useful Expression 必通實用句型

I've learned to find a good balance between [something] and [something].

我已經學會在〔某事〕和〔某事〕之間找到平衡。

Power Vocabulary 好用字彙

steady [`stɛdɪ] (*adj.*) 穩定的
feedback [`fid,bæk] (*n.*) 意見回饋
spreed out 散開
frustrated [`frʌstretɪd] (*adj.*) 挫敗的；失意的
cooperative [co`ɑpə,retɪv] (*adj.*) 合作的

accurately [`ækjərɪtlɪ] (*adj.*) 正確無誤地
multi-task [`mʌltɪ,tæsk] (*v.*) 同時處理多項事務
off balance 失去平衡
stressed out 緊張的；感到有壓力的
flexible [`flɛksəbl] (*adj.*) 有彈性的

✎ My own answer

Q7

What are your hobbies and interests?

你的興趣和喜好為何？

A1 有力簡答

Whenever I have free time, I like reading, doing yoga, and going shopping.

我空閒的時候，喜歡閱讀、做瑜珈和逛街購物。

A2 深入詳答

I tend to keep a balance between busy moments and free time, so I do have some interests. In my spare time, I try not to work on my computer too much, instead I like reading fashion magazines, yoga and meditation, and gardening. Doing yoga makes me feel relaxed and reading magazines boosts especially my imagination and creativity. I think that my interests help with positive thinking and self-development.

我傾向在忙碌的時候和空閒之間找到一個平衡，所以我的確是有一些嗜好。閒暇時我會儘量避免過度使用電腦，而我喜歡的是看時尚雜誌、做瑜珈和冥想，還有園藝。做瑜珈讓我感到放鬆，而看雜誌尤其可以增進我的想像力和創造力。我認為我的興趣有助於我的正面思考和自我發展。

Tips 面試一點通！

人一天的工作時間才占一天的三分之一，扣除睡眠，剩下的時間你都是如何安排的呢？老闆會想透過這樣的問題了解應徵者除了工作之外，是否有個人的興趣與嗜好。因為有正當興趣與嗜好的人，較可能培養出健康的身體與心智，且懂得適時放鬆調劑身心的員工，在工作上才不致輕忽倦怠。

Useful Expression 必通實用句型

Doing [something / activity] makes me feel [adjective].
做〔某事／活動〕讓我覺得〔形容詞〕。

Power Vocabulary 好用字彙

tend to 傾向於
yoga [ˋjogə] (*n.*) 瑜珈
gardening [ˋgɑrdn̩ɪŋ] (*n.*) 園藝
boost [bust] (*v.*) 增加；增進
creativity [krieˋtɪvətɪ] (*n.*) 創造力
self-development 自我發展

spare time 空閒時間 (= free time)
meditation [ˏmɛdɪˋtəʃən] (*n.*) 冥想
relaxed [rɪˋlækst] (*adj.*) 放鬆的
imagination [ɪˏmædʒəˋneʃən] (*n.*) 想像力
positive thinking 正面思考

🖊 My own answer

Q8

Describe a mistake you made before and how you overcame it.

請描述你曾犯過的一個錯誤和你如何化解它。

 Track 09

I once ignored customers' opinions and designed something that failed to satisfy my customers' needs.

我曾經忽略了客戶的意見，因而設計出不符客戶需求的東西。

A2 深入詳答

Well, one mistake in my career I've made so far is overlooking customers' real needs. When I worked at Essential Tech. as a R&D Engineer, I was assigned to develop some electronic products. My administrator urged me to talk to some potential buyers and check what their preferences were before designing any products. However, I was overconfident about my own ideas and just went ahead to make a device prototype without consulting customers' opinions in advance. It turned out that my ideal product was a failure in the market. But it was a good thing that I took proper actions afterwards. I asked the marketing department to conduct a focus group to collect customer feedback, and then modified some functions of the product based on customers' opinions. I was pleased that my product was eventually well accepted by the market.

嗯，到目前為止，我在職涯中犯過一個錯誤，那就是忽略了客戶的真正需求。我在 Essential Tech 當研發工程師時，曾被指派開發一些電子產品。我的主管叮嚀我在設計產品前先跟潛在客戶談談，看客戶喜歡什麼。但是，當時我對自己的點子太過自信，在沒事先詢問客戶意見的情況下就直接製作了產品的原型。結果我自認為的理想產品在市場上失敗了。但幸好我隨即採取了些適當的行動。我請行銷部門辦了一個焦點團體訪談以收集客戶的意見，然後根據這些客戶的意見來修改產品功能。我很高興我設計的產品最後被市場接受了。

Tips 面試一點通！

藉由這個問題可以了解到一個人的 problem solving ability（解決問題的能力）如何。老闆會提出此問題，不僅是想知道應徵者會如何看待其所遇到的問題，更想知道的是，他或她如何運用自己的能力化解這個問題。不需揣測老闆想聽的答案，而誇大地講述超出自己能力範圍的事例。

Useful Expression 必通實用句型

I was overconfident about my own [ability] and [do something] without [doing something] in advance.

我對自己的〔能力〕太有自信，導致沒有先做〔某事〕就做了〔某事〕。

Power Vocabulary 好用字彙

overlook [ˌovɚˋluk] (v.) 忽視；忽略
administrator [ədˋmɪnəˌstrestɚ] (n.) 行政主管
preference [ˋprɛfərəns] (n.) 偏好；愛好
prototype [ˋprotəˌtaɪp] (n.) 原型
modify [ˋmɑdəˌfaɪ] (v.) 修改；更改

assign [əˋsaɪn] (v.) 指派
potential [pəˋtɛnʃəl] (adj.) 潛在的
overconfident [ˋovɚˋkɑnfɪdənt] (adj.) 過度自信的
conduct [kənˋdʌkt] (v.) 實施；處理
base on 以……為基礎

✎ My own answer

Q9

What have you learned from your mistakes?
你從所犯的錯誤學到什麼？

A1 有力簡答　（承上題，以研發工程師為例）　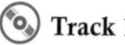 **Track 10**

From that mistake, I've learned that a good product R&D person should design products based on customers' real demands.

從這個錯誤，我學到了一個好的產品研發員應該按照客戶的實際需要來設計產品。

A2 深入詳答

After the mistake I just mentioned, I learned that I need to always be customer-focused. As we all know, "The customer is king." Companies need to maintain a competitive advantage, so we must create a customer-oriented culture. Now when I am designing new products, I always think twice about how the newly designed product can satisfy our customers' needs. Not only do I welcome feedback from clients more, but I also put myself in clients' shoes when doing my job.

在上述提到的錯誤之後，我學到的是要時時以客戶為中心。我們都知道，客戶是我們的衣食父母。公司必須維持競爭優勢，因此我們必須創造一個以客戶為導向的文化。現在，當我在設計新產品時，我都會思考新設計的產品如何能滿足客戶的需求。我不僅更歡迎客戶給我意見回饋，工作時也能設身處地為客戶著想了。

Tips 面試一點通！

只要是人就無可避免會犯錯，犯錯無妨，重要的是在修正錯誤之後是否能記取教訓，不再重蹈覆轍。換言之，老闆想從應徵者的答案中聽出他或她學到了什麼，今後也較有可能不會再犯相同的錯誤。

Useful Expression 必通實用句型

As long as I want to achieve [something], I must [do something].

只要是我想達成〔某事〕，我就必須〔做某事〕。

Power Vocabulary 好用字彙

mention [`mɛnʃən] (v.) 提及
competitive advantage 競爭優勢
customer-oriented 客戶導向的

✎ My own answer

Q10

Are you willing to travel? / Are you willing to relocate?

你是否願意出差？／你是否願意被調派到其他地區？

A1 有力簡答 （以國外業務為例） **Track 11**

I am willing to travel since I understand the importance of visiting overseas customers regularly.

我願意出差，因為我理解定期拜訪國外客戶的重要性。

A2 深入詳答

I am willing to travel since I totally understand the importance of visiting customers regularly to satisfy their requests. As a matter of fact, when I worked at A-Media Inc, I traveled to Korea once a quarter to develop long-term relationships with Korean buyers. And it is only through this relationship that customer loyalty can be established and financial growth can occur for both my clients and A-Media Inc.

我願意出差，因為我非常了解定期拜訪客戶並滿足他們要求的重要性。事實上，當我在 A-Media 公司上班時，我每季都會去韓國一次，為的就是要跟韓國買主建立長期的關係。也只有在這種關係上，客戶忠誠度才得以建立，客戶和 A-Media 公司的業績也才可能增長。

Tips 面試一點通！

全球化的結果使得很多公司都在世界各地設立分部，因此，員工需要出差或調職的機會可能越來越多。老闆想知道應徵者是否可以配合工作出差或調職，還是會因家庭因素受到牽絆？應徵者可以按照自己的實際狀況實話實說。

Useful Expression 必通實用句型

I am willing to [do something] since I totally understand the importance of [doing something] regularly.

我願意〔做某事〕，因我完全了解定期〔做某事〕的重要性。

Power Vocabulary 好用字彙

regularly [ˋrɛgjələlɪ] (*adv.*) 定期地
once a quarter 每季一次
loyalty [ˋlɔɪəltɪ] (*n.*) 忠誠度
occur [əˋkɝ] (*v.*) 發生；產生

request [rɪˋkwɛst] (*n.*) 要求
long-term relationship 長期關係
establish [əˋstæblɪʃ] (*v.*) 建立

✎ My own answer

Q11

What motivates you to do your best on the job?

什麼誘因會讓你在工作上全力以赴？

Well, I enjoy the sense of self-satisfaction I get after completing a tough task, so I would say the sense of pride motivates me to perform my best.

我喜歡完成艱困任務之後的成就感，所以我認為，榮譽感激勵我要全力以赴。

A2 深入詳答

Well, let me think for a bit. I would say that I am a self-motivated person so I don't require much external motivation. I work not only for paychecks, but more importantly, I work to get a sense of pride. I truly enjoy the satisfaction of achieving goals that go beyond expectations. And of course, I also like to be praised for my good work, but I know that the real reward comes when I complete important projects and realize that I have dedicated my best efforts to these projects.

嗯，讓我想想。我認為我本身是自我激勵型的人，不需要太多的外在誘因刺激。我工作不是只為了薪水，更重要的是，我想藉由工作得到榮譽感。我非常喜歡工作成果超出預期的那種滿足。當然，因為工作表現好而得到讚賞我也會很高興，但是我知道真正的回報是在完成重要案子，並體認自己全然投入其中之後到來。

Tips 面試一點通！

老闆想知道應徵者是為了什麼而工作，如同前述面試策略中提到的，回答時不要僅以自身利益為考量點，而要強調自己從工作上得到的成就感對公司也是有幫助的。

Useful Expression 必通實用句型

I would say that I am a [adjective] type of person.
我認為我是一個〔形容詞〕型的人。

Power Vocabulary 好用字彙

self-motivated [ˋsɛlf motɪvetɪd] (*adj.*) 自我激勵的
motivation [ˌmotəˋveʃən] (*n.*) 誘因；刺激
satisfaction [ˌsætɪsˋfækʃən] (*n.*) 滿足
expectation [ˌɛkspɛkˋteʃən] (*n.*) 預期
dedicate [ˋdɛdəˌket] (*v.*) 奉獻

external [ɪkˋstɜnəl] (*adj.*) 外在的
paycheck [ˋpeˌtʃɛk] (*n.*) 薪資支票；薪津
achieve [əˋtʃiv] (*v.*) 達成
realize [ˋrɪəˌlaɪz] (*v.*) 體認；了解
effort [ˋɛfət] (*n.*) 心力；努力

✎ My own answer

Q12

What are you passionate about?
你對什麼事有熱情？

A1 有力簡答 （以翻譯人員為例） **Track 13**

As an English major, I am passionate about translation and helping people communicate in different languages.

因為我主修英語，因此我對翻譯工作和協助人們用不同的語言溝通很有熱情。

A2 深入詳答

I am passionate about helping people communicate in different languages. I studied English as my major, so my ultimate goal is to use my professional translation knowledge to make a contribution to the Taiwanese people. You know, in this global village Taiwanese companies cannot afford to ignore global markets. So, I want to teach people in Taiwan to communicate with the world in English as well as to provide translation services to managers in international companies.

我對協助人們以不同語言溝通有很大的熱情。我主修的是英文，所以我最終的目標是要利用我專業的翻譯能力為台灣人做出一些貢獻。您也知道，在這地球村裡，台灣企業是無法對全球市場視而不見的。因此，我想教台灣的人如何以英語和世界溝通，也想為跨國公司的主管們提供翻譯的服務。

Tips 面試一點通！

當然，一個人要有傑出的表現，首要的就是要對他或她的工作充滿熱忱和興趣。若對工作沒興趣只是勉強地做，對個人與公司都是損失。因此，為了確保員工皆能人盡其用，老闆也會想了解應徵者的熱忱所在，以期日後分配工作時能善用其才能。

Useful Expression 必通實用句型

I am passionate about [doing something].

我對〔做某事〕有熱情。

Power Vocabulary 好用字彙

passionate [`pæʃənɪt] (adj.) 有熱情的
translation [træns`leʃən] (n.) 翻譯
global village 世界村
ignore [ɪg`nor] (v.) 忽視；忽略

ultimate [`ʌltəmɪt] (adj.) 最終的
contribution [ˌkɑntrə`bjuʃən] (n.) 貢獻
afford [ə`ford] (v.) 負擔

✎ My own answer

Q13

What qualities do you look for in a boss?
你心目中的老闆特質為何？

A1 有力簡答

 Track 14

In my opinion, a good boss should empower employees, provide them with useful suggestions, and possess strategic thinking ability.

在我來看，一個好的老闆應該要能授權給員工，提供他們有用的建議，並且要擁有策略思考的能力。

A2 深入詳答

All right, please give me a second to organize my thoughts. I think a good boss should allow employees the freedom to perform their jobs to the best of their abilities. And that's not all. A good boss should also provide employees with constructive suggestions so both employees and the organization can keep improving. Finally, I think a good boss should possess strong strategic thinking ability, so he can analyze market trends, competitor moves and customer demands in order to lead the organization in the right direction.

好的，請給我一點時間組織一下我的想法。我認為一個好老闆應該要能讓員工在工作上有發揮自己長才的自由。不只這樣，一個好老闆應該時時提供建設性的建議給員工，讓員工和公司都能不斷地進步。最後，我認為一個好老闆應該擁有很強的策略思考能力，如此他才能夠分析市場趨勢、競爭者動向和客戶需求，以帶領公司往正確的方向前進。

說到人格特質，一般人不免會想到 honest（誠實）、friendly（友善）、independent（獨立）等等，但這些特質可能在任何人身上都可以找得到。此題既然問的是「老闆」的特質，那麼答案就要偏向「領導人的特質」才行。面試官想藉機了解你認為的領導者或管理者應具備哪些特質。

Useful Expression 必通實用句型

A good boss should possess strong [adjective / noun] ability.
好老闆應該擁有很強的〔形容詞／名詞〕能力。

Power Vocabulary 好用字彙

empower [ɪmˋpauɚ] (v.) 授權
organize [ˋɔrgˌnaɪz] (v.) 組織
freedom [ˋfridəm] (n.) 自由
strategic thinking 策略思考
competitor [kəmˋpɛtətɚ] (n.) 競爭者

possess [pəˋzɛs] (v.) 擁有
thought [θɔt] (n.) 想法
constructive [kənˋstrʌktɪv] (adj.) 有建設性的
analyze [ˋænḷˌaɪz] (v.) 分析
direction [dəˋrɛkʃən] (n.) 方向

✎ My own answer

Q14

How do you determine priorities in scheduling your time?

在規劃時間時你如何決定事情的重要順序？

A1 有力簡答  Track 15

I concentrate on the most urgent and important issues, which helps me avoid distractions.

我會專注在最緊急且重要的事務上，這樣有助於我避免被其他事分心。

A2 深入詳答

In college I took a time-management course and learned to prioritize all tasks on the "Urgent / Important Matrix" tool. I now use the tool to help me look at my task list and quickly prioritize the matters I should focus on. I always focus on the urgent and important issues first and make sure that I am working towards my goals, and try to avoid distractions that do not contribute to my desired outcomes. Of course, some issues cannot be foreseen or avoided, so I also allow sufficient time in my schedule to deal with unexpected situations.

在大學時我修過時間管理的課程，並學到利用「緊急／重要矩陣」工具來安排工作的優先順序。現在我也利用此工具來協助我安排工作表，可以很快地將需要注意的重要事項優先排出。 我總會先將焦點放在緊急且重要的事務上，並確認自己努力地邁向目標，我也會避開那些對我想要的結果沒有助益卻會讓我分心的事物。當然，有些事無法預期或事先避免，所以我都會預留充分的時間以處理不可預期的狀況。

Tips 面試一點通！

在商業界，time management（時間管理）是一項很重要的技巧，老闆想藉由此問題得知應徵者如何分配時間，更重要的是，如何在有限的時間內將重要的工作優先處理完畢。

Useful Expression 必通實用句型

I always focus on [something] first and make sure that I am working toward my goals.

我總會先將焦點放在先〔某事〕上，並確認自己努力邁向目標。

Power Vocabulary 好用字彙

concentrate [`kɑnsɛn,tret] (v.) 集中
avoid [ə`vɔɪd] (v.) 避免
prioritize [praɪ`ɔrə,taɪz] (v.) 按優先順序處理
contribute [kən`trɪbjut] (v.) 貢獻
outcome [`aut,kʌm] (n.) 結果
sufficient [sə`fɪʃənt] (adj.) 足夠的

urgent [`ɜdʒənt] (adj.) 緊急的
distraction [dɪ`stræʃən] (n.) 分心；分心事物
focus [`fokəs] (v.) 集中焦點
desired [dɪ`zaɪrd] (adj.) 想要的；渴望的
foresee [for`si] (v.) 預見
unexpected [ʌnɪk`spɛktɪd] (adj.) 無預期的

✎ My own answer

Q15

What do you usually do during the weekend?
你週末通常會做些什麼？

 Track 16

During the weekend, I like to go swimming, visit friends, or just walk around my neighborhood.

週末時，我喜歡去游泳、拜訪朋友，或就在住家附近走走。

I usually try to relax on weekends so I can kind of recharge myself for the next week. I often go to the swimming pool in my neighborhood—I like swimming. Sometimes, I go to the local sauna. And I sometimes visit my friends, go to the cinema, and walk around Taipei on Saturday. On Sunday, I just like to stay at home and prepare for work the next day.

週末時我通常會試著放鬆自己，以便為自己充點電為下週做好準備。我時常去住家附近的游泳池——我喜歡游泳。有時候我會去附近的三溫暖。週六我有時會去拜訪朋友、看電影或就在台北附近走走。週日的話，我喜歡待在家裡，為第二天的工作做些準備。

Tips 面試一點通！

休息是爲了走更遠的路，一心埋頭工作而把自己逼得很緊繃的人工作效率肯定不佳。這個問題是爲了了解應徵者是否懂得適時放鬆、是否會善用週末做些有益身心的活動。

Useful Expression 必通實用句型

During the weekend I like to [do something].

週末時，我喜歡〔做某事〕。

Power Vocabulary 好用字彙

recharge [riˋtʃɑrdʒ] (v.) 再充電
neighborhood [ˋnebə͵hud] (n.) 社區；鄰近地區
sauna [ˋsaunə] (n.) 三溫暖
cinema [ˋsɪnəmə] (n.) 電影院
prepare [prɪˋpɛr] (v.) 準備

✎ My own answer

Q16

What do you do to keep healthy?
你都做些什麼來維持健康？

A1 有力簡答

 **Track 17**

To keep healthy, I maintain good eating habits, sleep well, and exercise.

為了維持健康，我維持良好的飲食習慣、睡眠充足，也會做些運動。

A2 深入詳答

Well, I try to keep myself healthy. In addition to maintaining good eating habits and sleeping well every night, I also stick to doing exercise. I go to the gym regularly in order to improve my cardiovascular health. More importantly, I believe holding in emotions can lead to illness, so I try to express my emotions in appropriate ways and learn to just let things go.

嗯，我盡量維持自身健康。除了維持良好的飲食習慣和每晚睡眠充足之外，我也經常運動。我定期到健身房運動，以改善心血管方面的健康。更重要的是，我相信情緒積壓久了也會生病，所以我試著透過適當的方式來抒發情緒，也學習不要太鑽牛角尖。

Tips 面試一點通！

老闆詢問此問題，除了想知道應徵者喜歡的活動類型之外，也可以藉由答案來判斷應徵者是否有強建的體魄以應付工作上的壓力。

Useful Expression 必通實用句型

In addition to [doing something], I also [do something] to keep healthy.

除了〔做某事〕之外，我還〔做某事〕來維持健康。

Power Vocabulary 好用字彙

stick to 忠於；堅信
gym [dʒɪm] 健身房
cardiovascular [ˌkɑrdɪoˋvæskjulə] (adj.) 心血管的
hold in emotions 壓抑情緒
illness [ˋɪlnɪs] (n.) 疾病
express [ɪkˋsprɛs] (v.) 表達
appropriate [əˋproprɪˌet] (adj.) 恰當的

🖉 My own answer

Q17

What do people most often criticize about you?

你周遭的人都如何評論你?

 Track 18

A1 有力簡答

Some colleagues think I am a perfectionist and pay too much attention to details.

一些同事認為我是個完美主義者,太過於注重細節。

A2 深入詳答

Well, some colleagues think I pay too much attention to details. I don't mean to be a perfectionist, but I just want to make sure that my tasks are done accurately and meet my superior's expectations.

嗯,有些同事認為我太注重小細節。我並不是刻意想成為完美主義者,我是想確認我的工作都能精確地完成,並符合上司的期待。

Tips 面試一點通！

回答此題要小心點，因爲題目中的 "criticize" 一字含有負面的意思；換言之，似乎是要提出自己的缺點，或爲人所批評之處。回答此題盡可能簡短帶過即可，因爲說越多很可能會越描越黑。人有缺點是正常的，試著提出「不是那麼嚴重的」缺點來回應即可。

Useful Expression 必通實用句型

I don't mean to be a [certain type of person], but I just want to [do something] well.

我不是有意成爲〔某種人〕，但我只是想要把〔行動〕做好。

Power Vocabulary 好用字彙

perfectionist [pə`fɛkʃənɪst] (*n.*) 完美主義者
pay attention to 注意
accurately [`ækjərɪtlɪ] (*adv.*) 精確地
meet one's expectations 符合某人的期待
superior [sə`pɪrɪə] (*n.*) 上司

✎ **My own answer**

Q18

Do you prefer to work independently or as part of a team?
你比較喜歡獨立作業還是團隊工作？

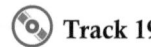 **Track 19**

A1 有力簡答

I like a mix of both. I like to work with a team to brainstorm new ideas together, while sometimes I like to work alone to get tasks done more quickly.

兩種方式我都喜歡。我喜歡和團隊一起工作，藉由腦力激盪想出好點子，不過有時候我喜歡獨立做業，如此可較迅速地把事情完成。

A2 深入詳答

Well, based on my own experience, I like a mix of both actually. I like to work with a team especially when all team members brainstorm new ideas together. I've learned a lot of good ideas from talking things out with other people. And sometimes I like to work alone on certain tasks as well because I think some tasks can be done better if one person is in charge of them. When arranging a seminar, for example, all team members need to get actively involved and make sure the seminar is successful. But, on the other hand, when working on a presentation slide file, the speaker of that specific session should be the person working on it.

嗯，根據我的經驗，我其實兩種工作方式都喜歡。我喜歡跟團隊一起工作，尤其是當團隊成員可一起腦力激盪構思出新點子的時候。跟他人討論工作讓我學到不少新想法。有時候我也喜歡獨立作業，因為我認為有些工作由一人負責會做得更好。比方說，在安排一場研討會的時候，所有團隊成員都要積極參與以確保研討會順利舉行。但是，反過來說，若是在準備簡報幻燈片檔案時，那麼這件事就應由該場簡報的講者負責。

Tips 面試一點通！

老闆可以透過此問題判斷應徵者的工作偏好。而事實上，在公司的運作中，需要獨立作業或團隊作業的情況都是有可能的。因此，最好是折衷回答，不要過度偏向一方。

Useful Expression 必通實用句型

When [doing something], all team members need to get actively involved.

在〔做某事〕的時候，所有團隊成員都要積極參與。

Power Vocabulary 好用字彙

mix [mɪks] (*n.*) 混合
alone [ə`lon] (*adv.*) 單獨地
seminar [`sɛnməˌnɑr] (*n.*) 研討會
presentation [ˌprizɛn`teʃən] (*n.*) 簡報
specific [spɪ`sɪfɪk] (*adj.*) 特定的

brainstorm [`brenˌstɔrm] (*v.*) 腦力激盪
arrange [ə`rendʒ] (*v.*) 安排
involved [ɪn`vɑlvd] (*adj.*) 有關連的
slide [slaɪd] (*n.*) 幻燈片
session [`sɛʃən] (*n.*) 講習會；（活動等的）時間

✎ My own answer

Q19

What type of work environment do you prefer?

你偏好哪種工作環境？

A1 有力簡答

 Track 20

I prefer to work in a safe and comfortable work environment. I also think that a company should be open to giving and receiving ideas.

我比較喜歡在安全和舒適的環境中工作。我也認為公司應該對意見的提出和採納採開放的態度。

A2 深入詳答

I think the fundamental characteristics of a good work environment are safe, comfortable and nice to work in. Also a company can create a great work environment by offering employees ongoing opportunities to develop new job-related skills. In addition, not only should a company provide feedback to employees about how they can improve, but a company should also welcome new ideas from employees.

我認為好的工作環境最基本的特徵是安全、舒適，而且會讓人樂意在其中工作。另外，公司可藉由不斷提供員工增進工作相關技能的機會，來創造出最好的工作環境。除此之外，公司不僅要時時提供員工關於如何在工作上更精進的意見回饋，也要能採納員工的意見。

Tips 面試一點通！

「工作環境」可指公司實體環境，也可以指無形的公司文化或工作氛圍，因此可以針對兩個方面都作一些說明。

Useful Expression 必通實用句型

Not only should S + V, but S should also V …
〔主詞〕不僅僅要……，還要……。

Power Vocabulary 好用字彙

fundamental [ˌfʌndəˋmɛntl̩] (*adj.*) 基礎的
characteristic [ˌkærəktəˋrɪstɪk] (*n.*) 特色；特徵
ongoing [ˋɑnˌgoɪŋ] (*adj.*) 進行中的；繼續的

✏ My own answer

Q20

How do you evaluate success?
你如何評斷成功？

A1 有力簡答

 **Track 21**

I think being successful is to try hard and achieve the goals I have set.

我認為成功就是努力嘗試並達成自己設定的目標。

A2 深入詳答

It's a wonderful question. As we all know, the definition of success is different for everybody, so there is no one best way to measure success. But for me, I think being successful is to achieve the goals or targets I have set. And in the workplace, I consider success as completing an assigned project or a task in the most efficient and productive way possible and within the stipulated time period. And of course, all these efforts are made in order to profit the company.

這是個很棒的問題。我們都知道，每個人對成功的定義不同，因此並沒有一個最佳的方式來評斷成功。但對我來說，我認為成功就是要達成我所設定的理想或目標。在職場上，我認為成功是在規定期限內以最有效率和產能的方式完成交辦的案子或任務。當然，所有這些努力都是為了讓公司獲益。

Tips 面試一點通！

每個人對成功的定義不同，有些人認為快樂就好，有些人想追求的是更好的生活等。老闆想藉此了解應徵者對成功的定義為何，並有什麼評估成功與否的標準。

Useful Expression 必通實用句型

The definition of [something] is different for everybody, so there is no one best way to measure [something].

每個人對〔某事〕的定義不同，因此並沒有一個最佳的方式來評斷〔某事〕。

Power Vocabulary 好用字彙

definition [ˌdɛfəˋnɪʃən] (n.) 定義

target [ˋtɑrgɪt] (n.) 目標

assigned [əˋsaɪnd] (adj.) 指派的

stipulated [ˋstɪpjəˌletɪd] (adj.) 規定好的

measure [ˋmɛʒ] (v.) 評定

complete [kəmˋplit] (v.) 完成

productive [prəˋdʌktɪv] (adj.) 生產力高的

profit [ˋprɑfɪt] (v.) 有益於

✎ **My own answer**

Do you consider yourself successful?

你認為自己是成功的人嗎？

A1 有力簡答 （以商管畢業生為例） **Track 22**

I think I am successful in terms of my MBA degree and English ability, but I always think there is still room for me to improve in the future.

以拿到企管碩士學位和英文能力來說，我認為我是成功的，但是我一直認為在未來我仍然還有進步的空間。

A2 深入詳答

I sometimes ask myself the same question. Well, in terms of my MBA degree and English ability, I would say yes. I am always interested in business and management, and I also believe English is an excellent tool to help me communicate with the world. So now I have my MBA degree and am able to use English fluently, I would say I have achieved my short-term goals. However, I do think that there is still room for further improvement, so I am not content with my current situation. Instead, I will keep trying and work hard to perform my best.

我有時也會問自己相同的問題。嗯，以拿到企管碩士學位和英語能力來說，我認為我小有成就。我一直都對商業和管理有興趣，我也相信英語是可以幫助我和世界溝通的絕佳工具。我現在擁有企管碩士學位而且能夠說流利的英語，因此我認為我已達到階段性的目標。不過我相信我還是有進步的空間，所以不會因現狀而自滿。相反地，我會繼續嘗試並努力做到最好。

Tips 面試一點通！

這是一個很有趣的問題，但回答時頗難拿捏。說自己已經成功了嘛，可能顯得過度自滿；說自己不成功，又顯得缺乏自信。所以可以強調自己已成功達成的目標或事件，並表明不會因此自滿，仍會不斷追求進步。

Useful Expression 必通實用句型

There is still room for [someone] to improve in the future.
〔某人〕在未來仍然還有進步的空間。

Power Vocabulary 好用字彙

room [rum] (*n.*) 空間
short-term [`ʃɔrt`tɝm] 短期的
content [kən`tɛnt] (*adj.*) 滿足的

fluently [`fluəntlɪ] (*adv.*) 流利地
improvement [ɪm`pruvmənt] (*n.*) 進步
perform [pɚ`fɔrm] (*v.*) 表現

✎ **My own answer**

Q22

What do your co-workers say about you?
你的同事如何看你？

A1 有力簡答 （以專案經理為例）
 Track 23

My co-workers describe me as a dependable, creative, and positive project leader.

我的同事說我是一個可靠、有創意並正面思考的專案經理。

A2 深入詳答

My co-workers describe me as a dependable, creative person with positive attitudes toward challenges. As a project manager, I have to ensure that what my team members do integrate with the big picture. Also I need to make tough decisions and meet deadlines. In addition, I always think out of the box and encourage my team members to be open to new ideas and don't get caught in assumptions. Finally, instead of trying to avoid problems, I encourage my team to see the opportunities in challenges and stay enthusiastic all the time.

我同事說我是一個可靠且有創意的人，對挑戰抱持正面樂觀的態度。身為專案經理，我必須確保團隊成員的所作所為都符合整體宏觀。我也須做困難的決策並在期限內完成工作。此外，我總是盡力跳脫原有的思考框架，鼓勵團隊成員要接受新的點子，不要局限在先入為主的觀念中。最後，與其試圖逃避問題，我鼓勵團隊要從挑戰中尋求機會並隨時保有熱情。

Tips 面試一點通！

從他人眼中來看自己是比較客觀的；當然，別人總不會都盡講些自己的壞話，回答此問題時還是應盡可能提出正面優點。除了提出別人對你的看法之外，不妨舉些實例來說明。

Useful Expression 必通實用句型

My co-workers describe me as a [adjective], [adjective] person with [adjective] attitudes toward [something].
我同事說我是一個〔形容詞〕、〔形容詞〕的人，對〔某事〕抱持〔形容詞〕態度。

Power Vocabulary 好用字彙

dependable [dɪˋpɛndəbl̩] (*adj.*) 可靠的

positive [ˋpɑzətɪv] (*adj.*) 正面的

ensure [ɪnˋʃʊr] (*v.*) 確保

tough [tʌf] (*adj.*) 困難的

think out of the box 跳脫思考的框架

enthusiastic [ɪnˌθjuzɪˋæstɪk] (*adj.*) 熱心的

creative [krɪˋetɪv] (*adj.*) 有創造力的

attitude [ˋætətjud] (*n.*) 態度

integrate [ˋɪntəˌgret] (*v.*) 整合；使成為一體

deadline [ˋdɛdˌlaɪn] (*n.*) 期限

assumption [əˋsʌmpʃən] (*n.*) 假定

✎ My own answer

Q23

Tell me about your dream job.

說說你理想中的工作。

 Track 24

I'd like to be in a job that I really enjoy. Also I want to work in a challenging environment and get a sense of achievement after completing a tough task.

我想要從事我真正喜愛的工作。另外，我想在有挑戰性的環境工作，並在完成困難任務之後獲得成就感。

A2 深入詳答

I happened to think about it as well just the other day. I thought I need to spend a very significant portion of my life working anyway, so I'd like to be in a job that I really enjoy. In addition to giving me a sense of achievement, I also think my dream job should be fun and challenging. As a marketing specialist I really enjoy planning product strategies. I always feel excited to get started in the morning and make sure I've accomplished something at the end of the day. Sometimes it's quite challenging to discover what consumers really like. But it's also fun especially when I can learn necessary marketing skills through real hands-on experiences.

前幾天我剛好也在思考這個問題。我想既然我生命中大部分的時間必須花在工作上，那就該做我真正喜愛的工作。除了得到成就感之外，我也認為理想的工作應該充滿趣味和挑戰性。身為行銷專員，我很喜歡規劃產品策略。每天早上我都會迫不及待想開始工作，而下班時我一定會確任完成某些事。有時，要找出客戶的喜好相當困難，但是也很有趣，尤其是在親自作業中學到必備的行銷技巧。

Tips 面試一點通！

被問及此題時，不少應徵者心中馬上會浮現「錢多、事少、離家近」這類答案，但如同我們在〈Section 1 你一定要知道的面試策略〉中討論過的，老闆並不是開慈善事業，爲什麼要提供這種好康工作給應徵者呢？因此，不要只想到你心中希望的答案，應從「工作的成就感」這類角度切入，最好能舉出實例說明，讓對方覺得雇用你是個最佳抉擇。

Useful Expression 必通實用句型

As a [job title] I really enjoy [doing something].
身爲一個〔頭銜〕我真的很喜歡〔做某事〕。

Power Vocabulary 好用字彙

portion [`porʃən] (n.) 部分

challenging [`tʃælɪndʒɪŋ] (adj.) 有挑戰性的

strategy [`strætədʒɪ] (n.) 策略

hands-on [`hændz`ɑn] 親自動手作的；躬親的

achievement [ə`tʃivmənt] (n.) 達成；成就

specialist [`spɛʃəlɪst] (n.) 專員；專家

accomplish [ə`kɑmplɪʃ] (v.) 完成；實現

✎ My own answer

Q24

What kind of person would you refuse to work with?

你拒絕跟哪種人共事？

A1 有力簡答 **Track 25**

I don't really like working with irresponsible, selfish colleagues, and people who don't cooperate with other team members.

我不太喜歡跟不負責任、自私的同事，和不與其他團隊成員合作的人共事。

A2 深入詳答

Well, based on my own experience, there are difficult colleagues in the office and I've encountered some of them. I don't really like working with irresponsible people, you know, people who don't show up for meetings and even if they show up, they don't contribute ideas, and people who don't turn their work in as scheduled. In addition, I don't want to work with selfish colleagues either. Some colleagues stick to their own opinions and refuse to collaborate with other team members, and in that case, it prevents the whole team from getting a consensus.

嗯，根據我自己的經驗，在辦公室總會有難相處的同事，而我自己也遇過一些。我不太喜歡跟沒有責任感的人共事，你知道的，就是那些開會都不出現，或即便出現了也不貢獻意見的人，還有那些不按進度完成工作的人。另外，我也無法跟自私的同事共事。有些同事太堅持己見，也不跟其他團隊成員合作，這樣會讓團體無法達成共識。

Tips 面試一點通！

辦公室內什麼樣的人都有，因此不免會發生各種狀況。老闆提此問題，除了能夠知道應徵者不喜歡哪種類型的人之外，也可以看出應徵者較重視的工作價值為何。比方說，若應徵者回答不喜歡跟「不負責任」的人共事，那麼這意味著應徵者頗重「責任感」。

Useful Expression 必通實用句型

I don't really like working with [adjective] colleagues, and people who don't [do something].

我不是很喜歡跟〔形容詞〕同事和不〔做某事〕的人共事。

Power Vocabulary 好用字彙

irresponsible [ˌɪrɪˋspɑnsəbl] (adj.) 不負責任的

difficult [ˋdɪfəkəlt] (adj.) 難相處的；不隨和的

contribute [kənˋtrɪbjut] (v.) 貢獻

refuse [rɪˋfjuz] (v.) 拒絕

prevent [prɪˋvɛnt] (v.) 防止；阻礙

colleague [ˋkɑlig] (n.) 同事

encounter [ɪnˋkaʊntə] (v.) 遇到

stick to 堅持；信守

collaborate [kəˋlæbəˌret] (v.) 合作

consensus [kənˋsɛnsəs] (n.) 共識

✎ My own answer

Q25

What kind of person would you prefer to work with?

你偏好跟哪種人共事？

A1 有力簡答

I prefer to work with co-workers who are hardworking, trustworthy, and willing to help others.

我比較喜歡跟勤奮、值得信賴和願意助人的同事共事。

A2 深入詳答

I prefer to work with co-workers who are hardworking, trustworthy, and willing to help others. I think hardworking people always devote themselves to the work and ensure that the work can be done effectively. In addition, trustworthiness is a necessary trait of an office worker. Since in a workplace environment there must be some sorts of confidential information, a trustworthy worker will not spread it out of the office. Finally, as I mentioned earlier, I don't want to work with selfish people. Instead I prefer to work with co-workers who are willing to provide assistance to others and mentor others through the hard times.

我比較喜歡和勤奮、值得信賴和願意助人的同事共事。我認為勤奮的人總是全力投入工作，並確認工作能有效率地完成。此外，值得信賴也是辦公室員工必要的特質。因為在工作場合免不了會有些機密資料，一個值得信賴的員工不會將之隨意散布出去。最後，如同我先前提到的，我不願意跟自私的人共事，我比較喜歡跟願意提供他人協助和在困難時能給予他人意見的同事工作。

Tips 面試一點通！

承上題，老闆當然也想知道應徵者會想跟哪一類的人共事，所謂「物以類聚」，由此題的答案也可聽出應徵者是具備哪種人格特質的人。

Useful Expression 必通實用句型

I prefer to work with co-workers who are [adjective], [adjective], and willing to [do something].
我比較喜歡跟〔形容詞〕、〔形容詞〕和願意〔做某事〕的人共事。

[Characteristic] is a necessary trait of an office worker.
〔某特質〕是一個辦公室員工必須具備的特質。

Power Vocabulary 好用字彙

hardworking [ˌhɑrdˋwɜkɪŋ] (adj.) 勤勉的
devote [dɪˋvot] (v.) 奉獻
trait [tret] (n.) 特質
spread [sprɛd] (v.) 散布；傳播
mentor [ˋmɛntə] (v.) 給意見；指導

trustworthy [ˋtrʌstˌwɜðɪ] (adj.) 可信任的
trustworthiness [ˋtrʌstˌwɜðɪnɪs] (n.) 可靠
confidential [ˌkɑnfəˋdɛnʃəl] (adj.) 機密的
assistance [əˋsɪstəns] (n.) 協助

✎ My own answer

Q 26

In what summer jobs have you been most interested? Why?

你做過最感興趣的暑期打工為何？原因為何？

A1 有力簡答 （以參加夏令營獲得領導經驗為例）

 Track 27

During my senior year in college, I worked as a summer camp counselor. It was an interesting experience because I had fun with children, made new friends, and learned leadership skills.

在大四時，我當過夏令營的指導員。那是一個有趣的經驗，因為我和小朋友一起玩得很開心，也結交了新朋友，還學到領導技巧。

A2 深入詳答

During my senior year in college, I worked as a summer camp counselor. I led a group of eight children roasting chickens, crafting tools, and learning to pitch a tent. My responsibilities also included keeping campers on schedule with activities, taking care of the budget, planning events, and making sure everyone was safe and happy. I think that summer job was interesting because it was all about having fun with children, making new friends, and learning leadership skills as well. I also believe the administration experience I have will benefit your team and company.

在我大四時，當過夏令營的指導員。我帶領一組八個小朋友，跟他們一起烤雞、做工藝，並學習搭帳篷。我的責任範圍還包括確保參加夏令營的小朋友都跟上活動時程、管理經費、規劃活動，並確認每個人都能安全和盡興。我認為這個暑期工作經驗很有趣，因為我跟小朋友一起玩得很開心，也結交新朋友，還學到領導技巧。我也相信我的管理經驗會對貴公司有所幫助。

Tips 面試一點通！

大學生除了唸書之外，免不了會有一些到公司或業界打工或實習的經驗。雇主藉此問題除了可了解應徵者過去的打工經驗，也可判斷這些經驗是否對職務本身有幫助。應徵者的答案最好和申請的工作相關。比方說，要應徵「記者」，若有「撰稿」的相關經驗就有加分效果，若提到當過「褓姆」則可能沒有多大幫助。

Useful Expression 必通實用句型

My responsibilities included [something], [something], and [something].

我的工作職掌包括〔某事〕、〔某事〕與〔某事〕。

Power Vocabulary 好用字彙

senior [`sinjə] (*n./ adj.*)【美】四年級生（的）

counselor [`kaunslə] (*n.*) 指導員

roast [rost] (*v.*) 烤

pitch [pɪtʃ] (*v.*) 搭（帳篷）；紮（營）

budget [`bʌdʒɪt] (*n.*) 預算

benefit [`bɛnəfɪt] (*v.*) 有益於……

summer camp 夏令營

leadership [`lidəʃɪp] (*n.*) 領導（能力）；統御

craft [kræft] (*v.*) 做手工藝

tent [tɛnt] (*n.*) 帳篷

administration [əd,mɪnə`streʃən] (*n.*) 行政管理

✎ My own answer

Q27

What has disappointed you about a job?

在工作中什麼事曾讓你沮喪？

  Track 28

When the outcome of my job does not turn out the way I originally expected, I feel disappointed.

當我的工作結果不是我原本預期的狀況時，我就會感到沮喪。

A2 深入詳答

Sometimes I feel disappointed with my job when the outcome doesn't turn out the way I originally expected. For example, I once looked forward to reaching higher sales volume, but when I lost some important cases, I felt really disappointed. Well, I think the key point here is that there are always valuable lessons in every experience I have. I believe my most profound learning comes from situations that don't turn out the way I anticipated. So I usually don't stay disappointed for too long. Instead I focus on learning from a wide range of outcomes.

有時我會因為工作結果不是我原本預期的狀況而感到沮喪。例如，有一次我預期會達到更高的業績目標，但是在錯失幾個案子之後，我感到非常氣餒。嗯，我認為重點在於，從這些經驗當中我總是可以學到寶貴的教訓。我相信從結果不如預期的情況中所學到的教訓最為深刻。因此我通常不會沮喪太久，而會專注於從各種結果中學習經驗。

Tips 面試一點通！

工作上不會事事順心，一定會遇到讓人氣餒之事，因此這道題目只要依照自己的狀況回答無妨。但除了描述令人氣餒的事之外，也別忘表達後續採取的行動及學到的教訓。

Useful Expression 必通實用句型

I believe my most profound learning comes from situations that don't turn out the way I anticipated.

我相信從結果不如預期的情況中所學到的教訓最為深刻。

Power Vocabulary 好用字彙

outcome [ˋaʊtˌkʌm] (*n.*) 結果
turn out 結果是；證明是
originally [əˋrɪdʒənḷɪ] (*adv.*) 最初的
disappointed [ˌdɪsəˋpɔɪntɪd] (*adj.*) 失望的；沮喪的
look forward to 期望
volume [ˋvɑljəm] (*n.*)（生產或交易的）量；額
profound [prəˋfaʊnd] (*adj.*) 深刻的；深切的
anticipate [ænˋtɪsəˌpet] (*v.*) 期待
range [rendʒ] (*n.*) 範圍

✎ My own answer

Q 28 ▸

Give me an idea of how you spend a typical work day.

請描述你平日一天的工作排程。

  Track 29

I always come into the office early, review transaction **records of customers in the morning, and go out to visit customers in the afternoon.**

我總是很早到公司，上午的時候我會檢視客戶的交易記錄，下午則出去拜訪客戶。

A2 深入詳答

I would say I am a morning person and work more productively **in the morning. Getting up early is pretty** manageable **for me, so I always come into the office earlier than other staff members in order to avoid unwanted** distractions. **Before I start contacting customers, I review transaction records of each existing customer and prepare** proposals **for** prospectives. **I make on** average **20 to 25 phone calls to the customers in a morning. In the afternoon, I either go out to visit customers or stay in the office to attend sales meetings. Sometimes, I also attend** internal **trainings to learn more sales skills. Before leaving the office at 6 p.m., I get my sales reports ready for my manager to** review **and we talk about the tasks I need to focus on the next day.**

我自認是早晨型的人，早上的工作效率比較高。早起對我來說不是問題，所以我總是比其他同事更早到公司以避免不必要的干擾。在開始跟客戶聯絡前，我會檢視一下現有客戶的交易記錄，並準備企劃書給潛在客戶。我一個早上平均會打 20 到 25 通電話給客戶。下午我不是外出拜訪客戶，就是留在公司參加業務會議。有時我也會參加內部訓練，學習更多業務技巧。在六點下班前，我會準備好業務報告給我的經理審閱，並討論我隔天的工作重點。

Tips 面試一點通！

老闆想了解應徵者的時間管理能力，並得知他或她在一天之中何時工作效率最高。當然，回答時切忌流水帳式地敘述每日工作細節，只要大方向地說明一日的時間安排即可。

Useful Expression 必通實用句型

I am a [adjective] person and work more productively in the [time period].

我自認是〔形容詞〕的人，在〔時間〕的工作效率比較高。

Power Vocabulary 好用字彙

transaction [trænˋzækʃən] (v.) 辦理；交易
manageable [ˋmænɪdʒəbl] (adj.) 易辦到的
proposal [prəˋpozl] (n.) 提案；提議
on average 平均上
review [rɪˋvju] (v.) 檢視

productively [prəˋdʌktɪvlɪ] (adv.) 有成果地
distraction [dɪˋstrækʃən] (n.) 分散注意力的事物
prospective [prəˋspɛktɪv] (n.) 潛在客戶
internal [ɪnˋtɜnl] (adj.) 內部的

✎ My own answer

Q 29

Do you have any blind spots?

你有什麼盲點嗎？

A1 有力簡答

 Track 30

I would say that my blind spot is to take some things too personally in the office.

我認為我的盲點是，在辦公室我會將某些事情視為是針對我個人的。

A2 深入詳答

To be honest, I do have a blind spot. I sometimes take things too personally in the office. For example, during a meeting if my boss mentioned that a certain task should've been done better, I would think he was criticizing my performance. I also understand that it's all about business, nothing personal, but I just can't help wanting to take things personally. In order to make myself more aware of how my blind spot might impact my decisions, I ask some of my close colleagues to remind me of it all the time. In addition, I also watch my own thoughts and stay conscious of how I think.

說實話，我的確有個盲點。在辦公室我有時會把事情視為是針對我個人的。比方說，在會議中如果我老闆提到某項工作可以做得更好，我就會認為老闆是在批評我的表現。我也了解這是就事論事，無關個人，但是我就是會忍不住認為事情是針對我而來。為了讓自己更了解我的盲點可能會如何影響我的決策，我請一些跟我較親近的同事隨時提醒我。除此之外，我也會注意我自己的思維並時時留意自己的想法。

Tips 面試一點通！

一個人不可能完美無缺，只要是人就會有盲點，因此，遇到此類題目照實回答無妨，但是要注意，提及的內容必須與工作相關。另外，有盲點沒關係，但是否會採取哪些行動讓自己不受盲點的矇蔽，才是面試官在意的重點。

Useful Expression 必通實用句型

I would say that my blind spot is to [do something]. In order to make myself more aware of how my blind spot might impact my decisions, I ask some of my close colleagues to remind me of it all the time.

我認為我的盲點是〔做某事〕。為了讓自己更了解我的盲點可能會影響我的決策，我請一些跟我較親近的同事隨時提醒我。

Power Vocabulary 好用字彙

blind spot 盲點
criticize [`krɪtɪˌsaɪz] (v.) 批評
impact [ɪm`pækt] (v.) 影響
conscious [`kɑnʃəs] (adj.) 有意識的

personally [`pɜsn̩lɪ] (adv.) 個人地
performance [pə`fɔrməns] (n.) 表現
remind [rɪ`maɪnd] (v.) 提醒

✎ My own answer

What were the last three books you read?

你近日讀了哪三本書？

A1 有力簡答

 **Track 31**

Recently, I've just finished reading "*The Grapes of Wrath*" by John Steinbeck, "*The Wind in the Willows*" by Kenneth Grahame, and "*The Last Station: A Novel of Tolstoy's Final Year*" by Jay Parini.

最近我剛讀完史坦貝克寫的《憤怒的葡萄》、格拉姆所寫的《柳林間的風聲》，和帕里尼所寫的《為愛起程：托爾斯泰人生的最後階段》三本書。

A2 深入詳答

Well, that's an interesting question. I personally love to read the classics. Recently I have finished reading "*The Grapes of Wrath*" by John Steinbeck, "*The Wind in the Willows*" by Kenneth Grahame, and "*The Last Station: A Novel of Tolstoy's Final Year*" by Jay Parini. Through reading these books, not only have I learned useful English vocabulary, but I have also gained more understanding of what happened in the old times in the US, UK, and why people loved Tolstoy so much.

嗯，這是一個很有趣的問題。我個人喜歡讀經典小說。最近我剛讀完史坦貝克寫的《憤怒的葡萄》、格拉姆所寫的《柳林間的風聲》和帕里尼所寫的《為愛起程：托爾斯泰人生的最後階段》。透過閱讀這些書，我不僅學到實用的英文字彙，還了解到更多關於美國、英國在過去時代所發生的事情，以及托爾斯泰受人愛戴的原因。

Tips 面試一點通！

此問題乍聽之下似乎跟求職面談沒有直接的關係，其實不然。這是一個了解應徵者是什麼樣的人最好的問題。老闆想知道應徵者偏好閱讀哪方面的讀物，是管理方面、勵志方面，亦或是科技方面的？藉此可以對應徵者有更深入的認識。當然，應徵者只要據實回答即可。

Useful Expression 必通實用句型

Through reading these books, not only have I learned [something], but I also have had more understanding of [something].

透過閱讀這些書，我不僅學到〔某事〕，我也了解到更多〔某事〕。

Power Vocabulary 好用字彙

The Grapes of Wrath（書名）《憤怒的葡萄》
The Wind in the Willows（書名）《柳林間的風聲》
The Last Station（書名）《為愛起程：托爾斯泰人生的最後階段》
classic [ˋklæsɪk] (n.) 經典名著
vocabulary [vəˋkæbjəˌlɛrɪ] (n.) 字彙
Tolstoy [tɑlstɔɪ] 托爾斯泰（俄國文豪及思想家）

✎ My own answer

 **精選好用句型，一次入袋！**

　　學完本單元的高頻問題及擬答後，試著寫下自己的答案，最後再複習一次本單元的好用句型，有助於在面試時靈活套用，秀出最好的一面！

▶ 說明個人的優點和缺點

☐ **I consider my [adjective / noun] skills and [adjective / noun] ability my two strengths. As for my weaknesses, well, I have to admit that sometimes I pay too much attention to [something].**
我認為我的〔形容詞／名詞〕技巧和〔形容詞／名詞〕能力是我的兩大長處。至於我的弱點，我必須承認我有時候會太注重〔某事〕。

▶ 說明個人的工作強項

☐ **I would say that my strongest skill is [something].**
我認為〔某事〕是我的強項。

▶ 說明如何處理壓力

☐ **I manage stress well because I always prepare fully.**
我壓力管理得很好，因為我都會在事先做好萬全準備。

▶ 說明個人的工作風格

☐ **I keep a steady pace on my work, and ensure that all assigned tasks are done accurately. In order to keep improving, I welcome feedback from my managers and other colleagues.**
我在工作上採取穩當的腳步，以確保交付的任務都可以正確地完成。為了不斷進步，我也樂於接納主管和同事提供我的意見。

▶ 說明個人的興趣、喜好

☐ **Doing [something/activity] makes me feel [adjective].**
做〔某事／活動〕讓我覺得〔形容詞〕。

▶ 說明曾經犯過的錯誤

☐ **I was overconfident about my own [ability] and [do something] without [doing something] in advance.**
我對自己的〔能力〕太有自信，導致沒有先〔做某事〕就〔做某事〕。

▶ 說明對何種事物具有熱情

☐ **I am passionate about [doing something].**
我對〔做某事〕有熱情。

▶ 說明心目中理想老闆的特質

☐ **A good boss should possess strong [adjective / noun] ability.**
好老闆應該擁有很強的〔形容詞／名詞〕能力。

▶ 說明別人眼中的你

☐ **My co-workers describe me as a [adjective], [adjective] person with [adjective] attitudes toward [something].**
我同事說我是一個〔形容詞〕、〔形容詞〕的人，對〔某事〕抱持〔形容詞〕態度。

▶ 說明心目中的理想工作

☐ **I'd like to be in a job that I really enjoy. Also I want to work in a challenging environment and get a sense of achievement after completing a tough task.**
我想要做我真正喜愛的工作。另外，我想在有挑戰性的環境工作，並在完成困難任務之後獲得成就感。

▶ 說明偏好和何種特質的人共事

☐ **I prefer to work with co-workers who are [adjective], [adjective], and willing to [do something].**
我比較喜歡跟〔形容詞〕、〔形容詞〕和願意〔做某事〕的人共事。

▶ 說明個人的盲點

☐ **I would say that my blind spot is to [do something]. In order to make myself more aware of how my blind spot might impact my decisions, I ask some of my close colleagues to remind me of it all the time.**
我認為我的盲點是，在辦公室我會〔做某事〕。為了讓自己更了解我的盲點可能會影響我的決策，我請一些跟我較親近的同事隨時提醒我。

NOTES

Part 3
關於過去學校或工作的問題：表現／經驗

Questions about Education and Previous Work:
Performance / Experience

Q31

Why did you leave your last job? / Why did you quit your job?

你離開／辭去上一個工作的原因為何？

A1 有力簡答

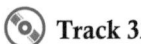 **Track 32**

I am eager to work in a more challenging environment where I can make better use of my skills and experience.

我很想要在更有挑戰性的環境工作，這樣我可以更善加利用我的技能與經驗。

A2 深入詳答

Well, I've been working for the same company in the same position for more than three years now, and it seems like there is not much room for me to advance with my current employer in the near future. So I am more interested in looking for bigger challenges and opportunities to apply my related sales skills and experience in a different capacity.

我在同一家公司擔任同個職位超過三年的時間了，感覺上在目前的公司短期之內不會有太多的晉升空間。因此，我想找尋更大的挑戰和機會，將自己相關的業務技能和經驗應用到不同職位上。

Tips 面試一點通！

離職的理由很多，但切記不要批評前公司的不是，或講前任老闆、同事的壞話，盡可能將焦點放在是經過自己深思熟慮才做出離職決定的整體原因。

Useful Expression 必通實用句型

There is not much room for [someone] to advance in the near future.

對〔某人〕來說在短期內沒有太多晉升的空間。

Power Vocabulary 好用字彙

quit one's job 離職 (=resign [rɪˈzaɪn])
room to advance 晉升空間
in the near future 近期
apply [əˈplaɪ] (*v.*) 應用

make use of 利用
current [ˈkɜnt] (*adj.*) 當前的
challenge [ˈtʃælɪndʒ] (*n./v.*) 挑戰
capacity [kəˈpæsətɪ] (*n.*) 職位；能力

✎ My own answer

Q32

Describe your work experience, and what is your most significant accomplishment?

請簡述你的工作經驗。你最大的工作成就為何？

A1 有力簡答 （以系統整合專案為例）

 Track 33

I would say that closing the CSI deal is my most significant accomplishment. Not only did I put a lot of effort into the case, but I also learned to communicate well with team members and balance different opinions. It was a valuable experience for me.

我認為完成 CSI 專案是我最大的成就。我不僅花了很多的心力在上面，也從中學到如何跟團隊成員溝通，並權衡不同的意見。對我來說那是非常有價值的經驗。

A2 深入詳答

I've been working in the CCI system integration company as a pre-sales representative for two years now. And for the most significant accomplishment, well, that would definitely be the CSI case which I just finished. It took me around six months to close the deal and I am pretty proud of it. For one thing, working on a big case like that required that I be very focused and goal-oriented. I worked closely with colleagues from sales and technical support departments and eventually came up with a suitable networking solution for the enterprise client to deploy. I definitely matured a lot working on that case. At the same time, I needed to have the ability to communicate with different types of people and to integrate constructive criticism into my planning. So I would say it was a huge growth experience for me.

我在 CCI 系統整合公司當業務代表已有兩年的時間。說到我最顯著的成就，嗯，那就非我剛完成的 CSI 專案莫屬了。那個案子我花了大約六個月才結案，為此我頗感驕傲。理由之一是，要處理像那樣的大案子我需要全神貫注朝目標前進。我和業務部和技術支援部的同事合作無間，最後設計出了一個最適合的系統連線方案讓企業客戶可進行作業。我確實從此案中成長不少。同時，我也需要具備和各式各樣的人溝通的能力，並將有建設性的批評建議整合到我的規劃當中。所以，我認為對我來說這是個非常重要的成長經驗。

Tips 面試一點通！

一般而言，老闆都會想了解應徵者的過往經驗和成就的事蹟。經驗部分簡述重點即可，不要細數流水帳。事蹟方面則應講述最顯著的成果，還有從中學到的寶貴經驗。

Useful Expression 必通實用句型

Working on a big project like that required that I be very [adjective] and [adjective].

處理像那樣的大案子，我需要非常〔形容詞（說明某狀態）〕和〔形容詞（說明某狀態）〕。

Power Vocabulary 好用字彙

significant [sɪg`nɪfəkənt] (*adj.*) 顯著的；重大的

integration [ˌɪntə`greʃən] (*n.*) 整合

goal-oriented (*adj.*) 成果導向的

come up with （針對問題）想出

enterprise [`ɛntəˌpraɪz] (*n.*) 企業；公司

mature [mə`tjʊr] (*v.*) 變成熟

criticism [`krɪtəˌsɪzəm] (*n.*) 批評；評論

accomplishment [ə`kɑmplɪʃmənt] (*n.*) 成就

representative [ˌrɛprɪ`zɛntətɪv] (*n.*) 代表

eventually [ɪ`vɛntʃʊəlɪ] (*adv.*) 最終

suitable [`sutbl̩] (*adj.*) 合適的；適宜的

deploy [dɪ`plɔɪ] (*v.*) 展開；布署

constructive [kən`strʌktɪv] (*adj.*) 有建設性的

✎ My own answer

Q33

Will you take extra work home with you?
你會將額外的工作帶回家做嗎？

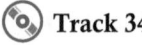

A1 有力簡答

If the situation requires that I take extra work home, I will do that.

如果情況需要我將額外的工作帶回家，我會這樣做。

A2 深入詳答

It really depends on the situation. I do understand the importance of meeting deadlines and getting jobs done on time. So when the situation requires I take work home, it's not a problem for me.

那得視狀況而定。我確實了解在截止期限前將工作完成的重要性。因此，如果情況需要我將工作帶回家做，我沒問題。

Tips 面試一點通！

這是見人見智的問題，試著簡短說明就好，不需要解釋過多。

Useful Expression 必通實用句型

I do understand the importance of meeting deadlines and getting jobs done on time. So when the situation requires I take work home, it's not a problem for me.

我的確了解在截止期限前將工作做完的重要性。因此，如果情況需要我將工作帶回家做，我沒問題。

Power Vocabulary 好用字彙

situation [ˌsɪtʃʊˋeʃən] (n.) 情況

importance [ɪmˋpɔrtn̩s] (n.) 重要性

extra [ˋɛkstrə] (adj.) 額外的

meet the deadline 趕上截止時間

✎ My own answer

Q34

What has been your experience in giving presentations?

你做簡報的經驗如何？

 Track 35

I did have some experience in giving presentations in college. Professors gave students opportunities to present ideas in front of the class. I felt nervous at first, but the more presentation experience I have, the better I can control my nerves.

在大學時我的確有一些做簡報的經驗。教授會給我們機會向全班同學提出自己的構想。剛開始我會覺得緊張，但是隨著做簡報的經驗越多，我也越能控制焦慮感。

A2 深入詳答

I would say that I've grown to be a competent presenter. One of my successful presentations took place at my university when I was responsible for presenting a new-product-development case for the class. After joining IT-Tech Company, I also had plenty of opportunities to present our IT products and solutions to clients. I felt a sense of fulfillment because not only did I engage the audience in what was being presented, but I also realized that the clients all liked my presentations and adopted the solutions I proposed. At first I felt nervous, but I found my own ways to harness my nerves and bring them under control. Now I am able to impress my audience with my calm delivery of a great presentation.

我認為在做簡報上已具有相當的能力。我最成功的簡報是我大學時做的，當時我負責向全班做一個新產品開發的案例簡報。加入 IT-Tech 公司後，我也有許多向客戶做產品和解決方案簡報的機會。我從簡報中得到成就感，我不僅針對簡報主題跟聽眾有很多互動，也發現客戶都很喜歡我的報告，且採納了我提出的解決方案。剛開始我也會緊張，但後來我找到控制焦慮感的方式。現在我可以穩當做一場讓客戶印象深刻的簡報。

Tips 面試一點通！

簡報技巧是想在任何公司有出色表現的人必備的基本能力。若有豐富的簡報經驗，在回答這個問題時自然能得心應手。但若沒有相關經驗，也應表明願意接受什麼樣的訓練或課程來精進這項技能。

Useful Expression 必通實用句型

The more [activity] experience I have, the better I can [do something].
隨著〔活動〕經驗越多，我也越能〔做某事〕。

One of my successful presentations took place at [place] when I was responsible for [doing something].
我最成功的簡報之一發生在〔地點〕，當時我所負責的是〔做某事〕。

Power Vocabulary 好用字彙

nerves [nɜvz] (n.) 憂慮；焦躁
take place 發生
fulfillment [fulˋfɪlmənt] (n.) 滿足；成就
audience [ˋɔdɪəns] (n.) 聽眾
propose [prəˋpoz] (v.) 提議
under control 在控制之下
delivery [dɪˋlɪvərɪ] (n.) 演講的姿態；傳遞

competent [ˋkɑmpətənt] (adj.) 能力強的
present [ˋprɪˋzɛnt] (v.) 做簡報
engage [ɪnˋgedʒ] (v.) 吸引住 (注意力、興趣等)
adopt [əˋdɑpt] (v.) 採用；採納
harness [ˋhɑrnɪs] (v.) 控制；駕馭
impress [ɪmˋprɛs] (v.) 使印象深刻

✎ My own answer

Q 35

What major problems have you faced and how did you handle them?

你遇到過最大的問題為何？你是如何處理的？

Once when I was in charge of arranging a seminar, I made wrong decisions and made some of our important attendees unhappy. I should've consulted with other colleagues for advice in order to prevent those mistakes from happening.

有一次我負責安排一場研討會，我做出了錯誤的決定，使得一些重要的與會者感到不悅。我當時應該先跟其他同事討論詢求意見，以預防那些錯誤發生。

A2 深入詳答

When I was working at Best-Systems, once I was responsible for an important Partner event and needed to divide approximately 100 CEO attendees into groups. I was aware of the "sensitive relationships" between these CEOs, so I arranged some CEOs to be seated in different groups. However, some colleagues suggested that the Partner event should be a good opportunity for people to mingle so even competitor CEOs should sit together. As the Partner event approached, I didn't insist on keeping some competitor partners apart on different tables. Then on the day of the event, I heard some complaints about seating arrangements and saw some unhappy faces. I learned my lesson from this experience, and knew I should be more careful when dealing with sensitive business arrangements in the future. More importantly, I learned that I needed to communicate with others more thoroughly in order to do the right thing.

當我在 Best-Systems 公司工作時，有次我負責一個重要的「夥伴」活動，須將大約一百位參加活動的執行長分組。我非常了解這些執行長之間的「微妙關係」，因此將一些執行長安排坐在不同小組。但是有些同事建議說，此「夥伴」活動是個讓執行長們互相交流的好時機，所以即便是競爭對手們也應該同坐。當時因為活動日逼近，我就沒有堅持將競爭對手分開坐。活動當日我聽到一些對於座位安排的抱怨，也看到一些不悅的臉孔。我從這次經驗中學到了教訓，了解今後在處理敏感的商務事宜時應更加謹慎。更重要的是，我學到若要把事情做對，我必須和他人做更完善的溝通。

Tips 面試一點通！

工作上不可能一帆風順，一定會有難題產生。針對這個問題，可精簡描述之前遇過的問題，但重要的是要提到當時處理的方式與因應的態度。

Useful Expression 必通實用句型

I should be more [adjective] when dealing with [something].
當處理〔某事〕時，我應該更〔形容詞〕。

Power Vocabulary 好用字彙

in charge of 負責……
attendee [əˋtɛndi] (*n.*) 出席者
approximately [əˋprɑksəmɪtlɪ] (*adv.*) 大約；近乎
mingle [ˋmɪŋgl] (*v.*) 使混合
approach [əˋprotʃ] (*v.*) 接近
thoroughly [ˋθɝolɪ] (*adv.*) 徹底地

seminar [ˋsɛməˏnɑr] (*n.*) 研討會
divide ... into 把……分成……
sensitive [ˋsɛnsətɪv] (*adj.*) 敏感的
competitor [kəmˋpɛtətə] (*n.*) 競爭者；對手
complaint [kəmˋplent] (*n.*) 抱怨

✎ My own answer

Q36

What do you like or dislike about your previous job?

你喜歡或不喜歡上個工作的什麼部分？

A1 有力簡答

 **Track 37**

I like all my colleagues since they are always optimistic. But sometimes it can be very busy in the office and I am too stressed out to sleep well.

我喜歡所有的同事因為他們總是很樂觀。但有時辦公室裏真的很忙，我會因為壓力過大而睡不好。

A2 深入詳答

I like the previous colleagues I worked with. They were all very positive and helpful. Of course sometimes the team encountered problems, but my colleagues stayed calm even in a difficult situation. And about the part I like least, well I was under a lot of pressure to meet deadlines. You know, there were always so many things happening, and sometimes it seemed like the phone never stops ringing. But still, through the hard work, I think I've built necessary skills to advance to the next level of challenge.

我喜歡之前和我共事的同事。他們都很正面也都樂於助人。當然，有時候團隊會遇到困難，但是我同事們即便在困難的情況之下也都會保持冷靜。至於最不喜歡的部分，嗯，要在期限前完成工作讓我很有壓力。您知道的，總是有層出不窮的事發生，有時就好像電話永遠響不停。但是，經過一番努力，我認為我已經具備了接受更高一層挑戰的能力。

Tips 面試一點通！

要討論喜歡的部分當然沒問題，但說到不喜歡的部分時，需注意評論不要過於負面，別讓人聽起來盡是在批評前公司的不是，而應將焦點放在是因為自己想尋求更大的挑戰這類因素上。

Useful Expression 必通實用句型

I was under a lot of pressure to [do something].
〔做某事〕讓我很有壓力。

Power Vocabulary 好用字彙

colleague [`kɑlig] (n.) 同事
previous [`privɪəs] (adj.) 之前的
encounter [ɪn`kaʊntə] (v.) 面臨；遭遇
advance [əd`væns] (v.) 進展；進步

optimistic [ˌɑptə`mɪstɪk] (adj.) 樂觀的
positive [`pɑzətɪv] (adj.) 正面的
pressure [`prɛʃə] (n.) 壓力

✎ My own answer

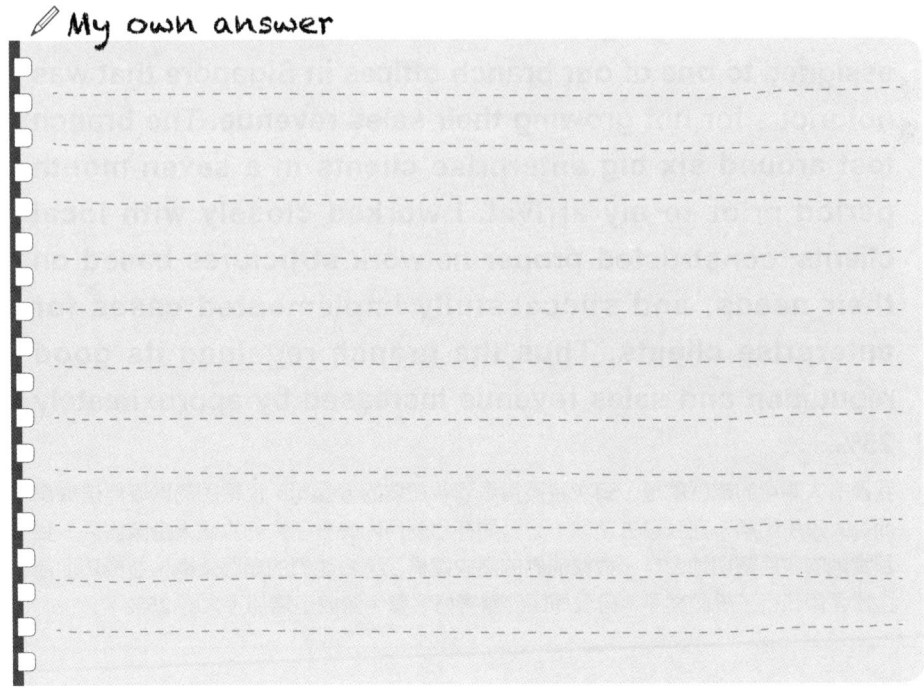

Q 37

What was the biggest accomplishment in your last position?

你上一個工作最大的成就為何？

A1 有力簡答 （以提升業績為例）

 Track 38

I was sent to our branch office in Singapore and helped them to win back major clients and boost the company's revenue by 25%.

我被派到新加坡的分公司去，協助他們贏回主要的大客戶，並大幅增加了公司的營收達 25%。

A2 深入詳答

The most satisfying accomplishment I had was that I was assigned to one of our branch offices in Sigapore that was notorious for not growing their sales revenue. The branch lost around six big enterprise clients in a seven-month period prior to my arrival. I worked closely with local clients, constructed proper network structures based on their needs, and successfully implemented cases for enterprise clients. Thus the branch regained its good reputation and sales revenue increased by approximately 25%.

我最令人滿意的成就就是，有次我被指派到新加坡的分公司，那裡因為營收無法成長而為大家所詬病。在我過去之前，分公司在七個月內失去了大約六個大企業客戶。我跟當地的客戶密切地合作，根據他們的需求建構了適合他們的網路架構，並成功地為企業客戶執行了幾個案子。分公司因此重獲好名聲，營收也增加了大約 25%。

這是所有產業老闆必問的問題。回答時可照實將自己做得好的部分精簡描述出來，但需注意要以明確的方式來表達。比方說，若只回答「我業績做得很好」，會讓人無法理解「很好是多好？」；若是能具體說出類似「我協助公司提升了 10% 的業績。」這樣明確的陳述，聽者就能有較清楚的概念。

Useful Expression 必通實用句型

I helped [company name] regained good reputation and boost company's revenue by [amount].

我協助〔公司名稱〕重獲好名聲，大幅增加了公司的營收達〔數字〕。

Power Vocabulary 好用字彙

branch office 分公司

boost [bust] (v.) 提高；增加

satisfying [`sætɪsˌfaɪɪŋ] (adj.) 令人滿意的

assign [ə`saɪn] (v.) 指派

enterprise [`ɛntəˌpraɪz] (n.) 企業

arrival [ə`vaɪvl] (n.) 到來

implement [`ɪmpləmənt] (v.) 執行

reputation [ˌrɛpjə`teʃən] (n.) 名聲

win back 重獲

revenue [`rɛvəˌnju] (n.) 收入；收益

accomplishment [ə`kamplɪʃmənt] (n.) 成就

notorious [no`torɪəs] (adj.) 惡名昭彰的

prior to 在……之前

construct [kən`strʌkt] (v.) 建構

regain [rɪ`gen] (v.) 重獲

approximately [ə`praksəmɪtlɪ] (adv.) 大約

My own answer

Q 38

What steps do you follow to study a problem before making a decision?

你在做決定之前會採取什麼步驟來研究問題？

 Track 39

A1 有力簡答

I try to identify the problem and possible factors first, then investgate causes and work on solutions to the problem.

我會先試著找出問題點和導致問題的可能因素，然後調查問題的起因並找出問題的解決方案。

A2 深入詳答

First of all, I write down the exact problem I encounter in detail, I identify who is involved, and where and when it occurs. And then I identify possible factors that contribute to the problem. Factors may be people involved with the problem, systems, equipment, materials, or external forces. I list as many factors as possible. After that I can investgate the most likely cuases further and work on possible and effective solutions to the problem based on the thorough analysis of the situation.

首先，我會將遭遇到確切問題的細節寫下來。我會確認相關的人員、問題發生的地點和時間等。接著，我會查明引發問題的可能因素，這些因素可能是相關的人、系統、設備、材料或外在條件。我會盡可能將所有的因素都列出來。之後，我就會依據對情況所做的通盤分析，進一步就最有可能的起因展開調查，以便找出可能和有效解決問題的方案。

Tips 面試一點通！

這是一個非常經典的問題。想在工作上一帆風順不遇到任何問題，幾乎是不可能的事。當問題產生時，重點是要如何解決。應徵者是否具備 "problem-solving skills"，以及遇到問題時的思考步驟，都是老闆據以評斷此人能否委以重任的關鍵因素。回答時可以「了解問題發生的根源」、「蒐集相關資訊」和「提供解決方案」等三階段來說明。

Useful Expression 必通實用句型

I try to identify the problem and possible factors first, then investgate causes and work on solutions to the problem.

我會先試著找出問題點和導致問題的可能因素，然後調查問題的起因並找出問題的解決方案。

Power Vocabulary 好用字彙

identify [aɪˋdɛntəˌfaɪ] (v.) 確認；識別
investigate [ɪnˋvɛstəˌget] (v.) 調查
encounter [ɪnˋkaʊntə] (v.) 遇到；面臨
contribute to 促成……
thorough [ˋθɝo] (adj.) 徹底的

factor [ˋfæktə] (n.) 因素
exact [ɪgˋzækt] (adj.) 確切的
occur [əˋkɝ] (v.) 發生
effective [ɪˋfɛktɪv] (adj.) 有效的
analysis [əˋnæləsɪs] (n.) 分析

✎ My own answer

Q39

How did your previous company achieve an advantage over its competitors?

你之前的公司如何發揮優勢並贏過競爭對手？

A1 有力簡答　（以流行服裝業為例）

 Track 40

My previous company sold business apparel. We focused our strategy on the superior quality of the products and after sales service we could offer.

我之前的公司銷售上班服飾。我們將策略重點放在提供優質產品和售後服務上。

A2 深入詳答

When I worked at Plus Fashion Co, we sold women's business apparel. We competed against our rivals to win customers on the basis of price, quality of products, the type of promotions, and the quality of service. So when we developed our business strategies, we focused on the superior quality of our clothing products and after sales service we could offer. We didn't go for the lowest price. Instead, our strategy was more directed towards getting the right match of quality and price. Also we had devoted a lot of time to demonstrating the quality of products and service that we could bring to our customers, and that was the company's main competitive edge.

當我在 Plus Fashion 公司服務時，我們銷售女性的上班服飾。我們以價格、產品品質、促銷方案和服務品質等要素跟對手競爭以贏得客戶。因此，當我們在發展競爭策略時，我們將重點放在提供優質服裝產品和售後服務上。我們不做低價競爭，我們的競爭策略較偏向在價格和品質之間取得最適當的搭配。另外，我們也花了很多時間證明我們可以為客戶提供高品質的產品與服務，這就是我們公司的主要競爭優勢。

Tips 面試一點通！

每家公司的競爭優勢不同，要在激烈的市場中勝出，有時不一定要跟競爭對手一樣發展同質性的產品，而是要有區隔策略，找到公司的「藍海」，如此才會找到公司的利基。老闆透過這個問題了解應徵者是否了解「企業應如何發揮自身優勢」的概念。當然，在面談之前就要對這些基本商務概念有一定的了解，回答時也可以舉實際的例子來說明。

Useful Expression 必通實用句型

When we develop our business strategies, we focus on [something] and [something] we could offer.

當我們在發展商業策略時，我們將重點放在我們提供〔某事〕和〔某事〕上。

Power Vocabulary 好用字彙

apparel [əˋpærəl] (n.) 服裝
superior [səˋpɪrɪə] (adj.) 優良的；較好的
rival [ˋraɪvl] (n.) 對手
go for 採用
devote [dɪˋvot] (v.) 貢獻
competitive edge 競爭優勢

strategy [ˋstrætədʒɪ] (n.) 策略
compete [kəmˋpit] (v.) 競爭
promotion [prəˋmoʃən] (n.) (商品等的) 促銷
match [mætʃ] (n.) 搭配；組合
demonstrate [ˋdɛmən͵stret] (v.) 證明；展示

✎ My own answer

Q40

Tell me a time when you had to deal with a difficult customer. How did you handle the situation?

請描述你跟難纏的客戶打交道的經驗。你是如何處理的？

A1 有力簡答　（以客服人員為例）

 Track 41

I receive phone calls from angry customers from time to time. To deal with these customers' problems, I focus on providing workable solutions and show my willingness to help them get their problems solved properly.

我不時會接到在氣頭上的客戶打來的電話。為了要處理這些客戶的問題，我會將重點放在提供客戶可行的解決方案上，並讓客戶了解我很願意協助他們圓滿地解決問題。

A2 深入詳答

As a customer-care representative, I need to deal with angry customers from time to time. One time I received a call from a furious customer complaining about a wrong delivery, and he was so angry and kept shouting that I didn't have a chance to talk. I understood that losing my temper wasn't the best way to get him to collaborate with me, so I kept calm, talked to him nicely, and gradually started getting his attention. Then instead of focusing on the situation I couldn't change, I focused on the workable actions I could take. I proposed some possible solutions for the customer and told him I was willing to work closely with him to get the problem resolved. Eventually the angry customer calmed down and collaborated with me to deal with the issue.

身為客服代表，我不時要面對一些氣憤的客戶。有一次我接到一個暴怒的客戶來電抱怨送錯貨品，他相當地生氣還不斷大聲吼叫，讓我毫無機會插話。我了解發脾氣無助於讓他跟我合作，因此我保持鎮定，跟他好好地說話，漸漸地取得了他的注意力。接下來，我並沒有把焦點放在無法改變的問題上，而是轉移到可採取的行動上。我提了幾個可能的解決方案讓客戶選擇，然後跟他說我很願意和他密切配合以解決問題。最後，那個氣憤的客戶終於平靜下來，跟我合作一起處理問題。

Tips 面試一點通！

任何企業都會遇到需要處理客戶抱怨的情況，因此老闆會想了解應徵者在面
對難纏客戶時的處理態度和應變能力。回答時應眞實地描述所遇到的狀況，
並說明後續處理的解決方式。

Useful Expression 必通實用句型

Instead of focusing [something], I focused on [something].
我並沒有把焦點放在〔某事〕上，而是把它轉到〔某事〕上。

Power Vocabulary 好用字彙

from time to time 不時；時常
willingness [ˋwɪlɪŋnɪs] (n.) 樂意
furious [ˋfjʊrɪəs] (adj.) 盛怒的
collaborate [kəˋlæbəˌret] (v.) 合作
gradually [ˋgrædʒʊəlɪ] (adv.) 逐漸地
eventually [ɪˋvɛntʃʊəlɪ] (adv.) 最終

workable [ˋwɜkəbl] (adj.) 切實可行的
representative [ˌrɛprɪˋzɛntətɪv] (n.) 代表
lose one's temper 發脾氣
calm [kɑm] (adj.) 鎮定的
propose [prəˋpoz] (v.) 提議

✎ **My own answer**

Q41

What were your responsibilities?
你之前負責什麼事務？

A1 有力簡答　（以規劃產品行銷活動為例）

 Track 42

I was in charge of product marketing. My duties included planning strategies, arranging activities, and writing marketing reports.

我主要負責產品行銷。我的責任範圍包括規劃策略、安排活動和寫行銷報告。

A2 深入詳答

When I worked at DigiTech Company, I was responsible for product marketing and developing strategies to increase product awareness and helping sales representatives to drive revenues. For the new product launches, I led a staff of six to create a series of readiness events, such as seminars, campaigns, and promotional activities. And then after the launch, I designed a tracking scheme to trace feedback from customers, compiled results, and reported the results to managers. Through participation, I personally have developed strong marketing skills, and received the GM Award for three consecutive years.

當我在 DigiTech 公司工作時，我負責的是產品行銷和開發策略以期提高產品的能見度，並協助業務代表增加營收。在新產品上市部分，我帶領一個六人小組規劃了一系列的預備活動，如研討會、推廣和促銷活動等。在產品上市之後，我設計了一個追蹤系統以取得客戶的回饋意見，在匯整好資料後將結果交給主管參考。透過親身的參與，我個人發展了很強的行銷能力，也連續三年得到「總經理獎」的殊榮。

Tips 面試一點通！

之前所負責的事務應徵者自己當然最為熟悉，只要據實以告即可。重點是除了講述負責過的事務之外，還可提到達成的事蹟與從中學到的經驗。

Useful Expression 必通實用句型

I was in charge of [something]. My duties included [doing something], [doing something], and [doing something].
我主要負責〔某事〕。我的責任範圍包括〔做某事〕、〔做某事〕和〔做某事〕。

Power Vocabulary 好用字彙

in charge of 負責
drive [draɪv] (v.) 驅動
launch [lɔntʃ] (n.) 發行；上市
seminar [ˋsɛməˌnar] (n.) 研討會
promotional [prəˋmoʃən̩] (adj.) 促銷的
scheme [skim] (n.) 計劃；系統
participation [parˌtɪsəˋpeʃən] (n.) 參與

awareness [əˋwɛrnɪs] (n.) 察覺；體認
revenue [ˋrɛvəˌnju] (n.) 收益
readiness [ˋrɛdɪnɪs] (n.) 準備就緒
campaign [kæmˋpen] (n.) (為某目的辦的) 活動
track [træk] (v.) 追蹤
compile [kəmˋpaɪl] (v.) 匯編
consecutive [kənˋsɛkjʊtɪv] (adj.) 連續的

🖉 My own answer

Q 42

What are the core skills needed to manage a team?

要管理好團隊的核心技巧有哪些？

A1 有力簡答 （以中階主管為例） **Track 43**

I think some key skills range from choosing the right people and deciding who does what to developing and motivating team members.

我認為從挑選對的團隊成員並決定誰來負責什麼事，到訓練及激勵團隊成員都應該是重要的技巧。

A2 深入詳答

Well, I think in order to manage a team well, some key skills range from choosing the right people, to communicating with team members, and motivating them. Let me give you an example. During the period with Rich shoe company, I moved from being a worker to a line manager. I needed to develop a new set of skills, and made use of new tools and techniques. All these have helped me with organizing, motivating, developing and communicating with my team. Not only do I think managing team discipline effectively is important, but I also want to make sure that I avoid some commonly made mistakes.

嗯，我認為要將團隊管理好，從挑選對的團隊成員到跟成員溝通並激勵他們都應該是重要的技巧。讓我舉個例子。當我在 Rich 皮鞋公司工作時，我從基層員工升到部門經理的位置。我需發展新的技巧並利用新的工具和方法。這些都有助於我管理、激勵、訓練團隊成員並和跟他們溝通。我不僅認為有效將團隊紀律建立起來是很重要的，我還希望確實能避免掉一些常犯的錯誤。

Tips 面試一點通！

除非是一人公司，否則在一般的公司環境下免不了要跟各式各樣的人共事。
老闆想了解應徵者是否能夠和他人愉快共事、是否有團隊合作的概念，或是
否具備管理團隊的技巧。回答的焦點當然要放在跟團隊成員合作愉快的例子
上，不要盡說些和團隊意見相左的不快經驗。

Useful Expression 必通實用句型

Not only do I think managing [something] effectively is important, but I also want to make sure that I avoid some commonly-made mistakes.

我不僅認為有效地管理〔某事〕很重要，我希望確實避免掉一些常犯的錯誤。

Power Vocabulary 好用字彙

range [rendʒ] (*v.*) 涉及
line manager 部門經理
discipline [ˋdɪsəplɪn] (*n.*) 紀律
avoid [əˋvɔɪd] (*v.*) 避免

motivate [ˋmotəˌvet] (*v.*) 激勵；激發
technique [tɛkˋnik] (*n.*) 技巧
effectively [ɪˋfɛktɪvlɪ] (*adv.*) 有效地
commonly [ˋkɑmənlɪ] (*adv.*) 通常地；一般地

✐ My own answer

Q 43

What was it like working for your previous supervisor?

跟你的前任主管共事是什麼感覺？

A1 有力簡答

 Track 44

It was a valuable experience working for my previous supervisor, Mr. Hart. He made decisions, identified problems, and found opportunities in a very professional manner.

我跟前主管 Mr. Hart 共事是很寶貴的經驗。他在做決定、找出問題以及開展機會上都很專業。

A2 深入詳答

When I worked at Brook-Hart Publisher, my supervisor, Mr. Hart, was one of the best supervisors I've ever had. He made decisions effectively, identified problems quickly, found opportunities successfully, and had excellent communication skills. All employees believed in him and trusted his decisions and actions. Working with Mr. Hart made me realize that I need to constantly look for ways to achieve more with the same amount of effort. I would say it was a very valuable experience working for him and I've learned a lot from him as well.

當我在 Brook-Hart 出版社工作時，我的主管 Mr. Hart 是我遇過最好的上司之一。他做決定時很有效率，可以很快地發現問題，成功地找到機會，也有很好的的溝通技巧。所有員工都信任他，相信他所做的決定和採取的行動都是正確的。跟 Mr. Hart 共事讓我了解到，我需要不斷尋求事半功倍的方法來做事。我認為與他共事是很寶貴的經驗，我從他身上學到很多。

Tips 面試一點通！

表面上看起來這是在問跟前任主管的共事經驗，似乎和新工作無關，但事實上，老闆想藉此了解應徵者看待人的態度。若應徵者盡是講述前任主管的壞話，由此可知應徵者心中充滿不平，即便是事過境遷，還是會以負面的心態看待事情。因此，回答時應持正面的態度，把重點擺在描述自前任主管身上學到的經驗或長處上。

Useful Expression 必通實用句型

It was a valuable experience working for my previous supervisor, [name]. He [do something], [do something], and [do something] in a very professional manner.

我跟前主管〔人名〕共事的經驗是很珍貴的。他在〔做某事〕、〔做某事〕以及〔做某事〕上都很專業。

Power Vocabulary 好用字彙

supervisor [͵supɚ`vaɪzɚ] (*n.*) 監督；上司
publisher [`pʌblɪʃɚ] (*n.*) 出版商
constantly [`kɑnstəntlɪ] (*adv.*) 不斷地
effort [`ɛfɚt] (*n.*) 努力；盡力

identify [aɪ`dɛntə͵faɪ] (*v.*) 指認；識別
realize [`rɪə͵laɪz] (*v.*) 領悟；了解
achieve [ə`tʃiv] (*v.*) 達成
valuable [`væljʊəbl̩] (*adj.*) 有價值的

✎ **My own answer**

Q44

Have you ever had difficulty working with a manager?

你和主管共事曾有過問題嗎？

A1 有力簡答 **Track 45**

Well, I have difficulty working with a manager who won't give his employees room to grow and the opportunity to develop their careers.

嗯，跟不給員工發展空間和拓展職涯機會的主管共事我覺得有些困難。

A2 深入詳答

Since I consider myself a rather ambitious person, I have difficulty working with a manager who won't step back and give his team members the space to get on and do their job. When I worked at EAU Corp. last year, there was a manager who didn't give employees room to grow and the opportunity to develop their careers. So I talked to the manager and stated that I wanted to know I was going somewhere and asked him to give me opportunities to prove myself. And then I achieved more goals with the manager providing the right kind of support.

由於我自認是一個頗有企圖心的人，因此和不放手讓員工表現和不能給予員工空間做事的主管共事我覺得有些困難。去年當我在 EAU 公司工作時，有個經理不給員工成長空間和拓展職涯的機會。我就跟那位主管談，表明我想確定自己能做出一些成績，並請他給我機會證明。之後，在這位主管提供正確的協助之下，我達成了更多的目標。

Tips 面試一點通！

這的確是個不易回答的問題。若回答說完全沒問題，似乎不太符合現實狀況。但若說和上司共事有很多問題產生，又會讓人覺得應徵者似乎很難相處。因此，回答時可以提一個和上司相處的小問題，比方說「對某個案子的期待不同」，但應將焦點放在解決方法上。

Useful Expression 必通實用句型

I have difficulty working with a manager who won't [do something] and [do something].

跟不〔做某事〕和〔做某事〕的主管共事我覺得有些困難。

Power Vocabulary 好用字彙

develop [dɪˋvɛləp] (v.) 發展
ambitious [æmˋbɪʃəs] (adj.) 有野心的；有企圖心的
career [kənˋrɪr] (n.) 職涯
prove [pruv] (v.) 證明
achieve [əˋtʃiv] (v.) 達成

✎ **My own answer**

Q45

What have you been doing since your last job?

從前一份工作離職後，你都在做些什麼？

A1 有力簡答

 Track 46

During the past three months, I did volunteering work in a local library, took computer design and English courses, and reevaluated what jobs are more suitable for me.

過去的三個月內，我在本地的圖書館當志工，還上了一些電腦設計和語言學習課程，也重新評估我自己比較適合做哪些工作。

A2 深入詳答

After I left Ross Publisher three months ago, I did quite a lot. For instance, I offered my services in a local library and volunteered to read children stories during the weekend. And I also used all the extra time on my hands to read a few books related to the publishing fields. I took the CAD design class I always wanted to do, and also got the TOEIC certification to make my resume stand out. Most importantly, I spent some time reevaluating who I really am, what exactly I want, and what jobs best fit my personality.

我三個月前離開 Ross 出版社之後，我做了不少事。比方說，我到本地的圖書館擔任志工並在週末唸故事書給小朋友聽。我也利用多出來的時間看了一些與出版有關的書籍，還上了我一直想學的 CAD 設計電腦課。同時，為了讓履歷表更出色，我也通過了 TOEIC 檢定考試。更重要的是，我花了一些時間重新評估自己是怎麼樣的人、我到底想要什麼，以及什麼工作最符合我的個性。

Tips 面試一點通！

若應徵者的履歷表上顯示自上個工作離職至找到下個工作之間有空檔時間，老闆可能就會想了解原因。不要只回答「想休息一下」等這樣模糊的答案，可以說明自己如何利用這段時間進修（如加強電腦技能或到國外進修英文等）。也就是說，要提出「休息是為了讓自己充電」這類答案才有加分效果。

Useful Expression 必通實用句型

I spent some time reevaluating who I am, what exacty I want, and what jobs best fit my personality.

我花了一些時間重新評估自己是怎麼樣的人、我到底想要什麼，以及什麼工作最符合我的個性。

Power Vocabulary 好用字彙

volunteer [ˌvɑlənˋtɪr] (v.) 擔任志工
publisher [ˋpʌblɪʃə] (n.) 出版公司；出版商
personality [ˌpɜsṇˋælətɪ] (n.) 個性；性格

reevaluate [ˌriɪˋvæljuˌet] (v.) 重新評估
certification [ˌsɜtɪfəˋkeʃən] (n.) 證書；檢定

✎ My own answer

Q 46

What academic classes and training courses have you taken that have prepared you for this job?

你之前上過什麼課或受過何種訓練讓你可勝任這份工作？

A1 有力簡答 （以科技產業為例）

 Track 47

I double-majored in computer science and strategic management in college. And, I have also taken some communication skills training courses.

我大學雙主修電腦科學和策略管理。我也上過一些溝通技巧相關的訓練課程。

A2 深入詳答

From my CV, you will note that I double-majored in computer science and strategic management in college. I have always believed that knowledge of computers and understanding of business analysis are equally important. It's worth mentioning that I have some experience working part-time at Hollett Corp. In addition, I have taken some communication-related training classes, such as presentation skills and negotiation skills. I believe this combination makes me a qualified technical manager.

您可在我履歷表上看到，我大學時雙主修電腦科學和策略管理。我一直認為電腦知識和對商務分析的了解同樣重要。值得一提的是，我有在 Hollett 企業兼職的一些經驗。另外，我也上過幾個溝通相關的訓練課程，比如簡報技巧和談判技巧。我相信這樣的組合讓我可以成為一位稱職的技術經理。

Tips 面試一點通！

每個人的專業領域不同，簡單描述自己所受過的訓練最為直接。但此題的要點在於「所受過的訓練如何有助於你勝任此項工作」，因此提到的內容應盡可能與工作相關。比方說，若應徵「工程師」職務，提到上過烹飪課程便毫無助益。反之，若應徵「國外業務」，則受過外語訓練或談判技巧訓練就絕對有加分的效果。

Useful Expression 必通實用句型

I have always believed that knowlodge of [something] and understanding of [something] are equally important.

我一直認為〔某事〕的知識和對〔某事〕的了解同樣重要。

Power Vocabulary 好用字彙

double-major 雙主修

CV 履歷（為 curriculum vitae 的簡稱）

combination [ˌkɑmbəˋneʃən] (n.) 綜合

strategic management 策略管理

negotiation [nɪˌgoʃɪˋeʃən] (n.) 談判；協商

qualified [ˋkwɑləˌfaɪd] (adj.) 合格的；可勝任的

🖉 My own answer

Q47

What do you bring to the table in terms of skills in customer interaction?

在跟客戶互動方面你最擅長的技巧是什麼？

A1 有力簡答 （以網路規劃產業為例）

 Track 48

When interacting with customers, I listen to what they have to say first and then design solutions based on their requirements. I also discuss project details with them and maintain a good relationship with them.

當我跟客戶互動時，我會先聽他們的意見，然後再根據他們的要求設計解決方案。我也會跟他們討論企劃的細節，並和他們保持良好的關係。

A2 深入詳答

Well, my current company designs computer network infrastructures for the manufacturing industry. It's a niche market, so in fact we have quite a limited number of customers. First of all, I have to listen carefully to what their requirements are. Our clients send us their network requirements and specifications and we design a network environment based on their needs. Also I make use of my communication skills in meetings. We have a lot of meetings at different levels—management level for deciding prices, structuring the project, and then technical teams get involved implementing the project. Oh, and I try to keep on friendly terms with the key people in our client companies, so I socialize a lot when I can.

嗯，我目前的公司做的是幫製造業客戶設計電腦網路基礎架構。由於這是個利基市場，所以事實上我們的客戶並不是很多。首先，我會仔細傾聽他們的需求為何。我們的客戶會先將網路需求和細項規格傳給我們，我們再根據他們的要求來設計網路環境。另外，我也會在會議中善用溝通能力。我們會舉行不同層級的許多會議，比方說跟管理階級討論價格的訂定、規劃專案，然後再由技術團隊規劃專案的執行。噢，我還會盡力跟客戶公司的主要人員保持友好關係，所以有機會我會多跟客戶互動。

Tips 面試一點通！

任何公司所提供的產品或服務都是為了要符合客戶需求，因此與客戶的互動能力就顯得格外重要。老闆會想了解應徵者將如何跟客戶互動、會使用哪些方法讓客戶買單等。回應這個問題最佳的答案就是時時以客戶的角度出發，為客戶著想。

Useful Expression 必通實用句型

When interacting with customers, I listen to what they have to say first and then [do something] based on [something].

當我跟客戶互動時，我先聽他們的意見，然後再根據〔某事〕來〔做某事〕。

Power Vocabulary 好用字彙

interact [ˌɪntɚˋrækt] (*v.*) 互動
maintain [menˋten] (*v.*) 維持
infrastructure [ˋɪnfrəˌstrʌktʃɚ] (*n.*) 基礎架構
niche market 利基市場
involve [ɪnˋvɑlv] (*v.*) 參與；關連
socialize [ˋsoʃəˌlaɪz] (*v.*) 交際；社交

requirement [rɪˋkwaɪrmənt] (*n.*) 需求；要求
current [ˋkɝənt] (*adj.*) 目前的；現在的
manufacturing industry 製造業
specification [ˌspɛsəfəˋkeʃən] (*n.*) 規格；明細單
implement [ˋɪmpləmənt] (*v.*) 實施；執行

✏ My own answer

Q48

What specific experiences do you have in conflict resolution?

你解決衝突的具體經驗為何？

 Track 49

When encountering conflict, I try to be direct, clarify what is going on, and proactively work with team members to come up with appropriate solutions.

當有衝突產生時，我會試著表明態度、弄清楚狀況，並積極主動地跟團隊成員合作找出適當的解決之道。

A2 深入詳答

Well, I would say conflict can be pretty much inevitable when people work in a team. Instead of ignoring it or blaming someone for it, I try to be direct, clarify what is going on, and proactively work with others to reach a proper resolution. For example, when I was with Collins Soft-Drink Company, some of the team members believed the best way to promote our new beverage products was through a TV campaign, while some others insisted that internet advertising was the way to go. So conflict followed. In order to resolve the conflict, I invited all team members to sit down and communicate, let everyone clarify his position and list facts underlining it, and then analyzed and compared each position before all members could reach a final agreement.

嗯，我認為在團隊中與他人共事，衝突很難避免。遇到衝突時我不會忽略它或怪罪他人，我會試著表明態度、弄清楚狀況，並主動和其他人合作以找出適當的解決之道。比方說，當我在 Collins 飲料公司上班時，有一些同事認為電視廣告是推廣新飲料產品的最佳方式，但是其他幾位同事認為網路廣告才是最有效的。接著就發生了衝突。為了解決衝突，我邀請團隊所有人坐下來好好溝通，讓每個人說明自己的立場並列出事實根據，接著分析和比較各別的立場，使得最後所有成員可以達成共識。

Tips 面試一點通！

與人共事偶有衝突是難免的，重點在於如何解決與後續的處理。回答時，可根據應徵者個人的經驗描述，但無須強調誰對誰錯，而應將焦點放在化解問題的方法上。

Useful Expression 必通實用句型

In order to resolve the conflict, I [do something], [do something], and then [do something].

為了化解衝突，我〔做某事〕、〔做某事〕，接著再〔做某事〕。

Power Vocabulary 好用字彙

direct [də`rɛkt] (*adj.*) 直接的
proactively [pro`æktɪvlɪ] (*adv.*) 主動地；積極地
solution [sə`luʃən] (*n.*) 解決；解答
ignore [ɪg`nor] (*v.*) 忽略
campaign [kæm`pen] (*n.*) 活動
reach an agreement 達成共識

clarify [`klærə͵faɪ] (*v.*) 澄清；闡明
appropriate [ə`proprɪ͵et] (*adj.*) 適當的
inevitable [ɪn`ɛvətəbl] (*adj.*) 不可避免的
blame [blem] (*v.*) 怪罪
position [pə`zɪʃən] (*n.*) 立場

✐ **My own answer**

Q49

Why have you decided to seek a position in this field?

什麼原因驅使你往這領域發展？

A1 有力簡答 （以觀光領域為例）

 **Track 50**

Since my parents are both tour guides, I am influenced by them and always interested in learning more about this world. That's why I've always wanted to work in the tourist industry.

因為我父母都是導遊，我受到他們的影響，一直對多了解這個世界非常感興趣。這就是我一直想進入旅遊業這個領域的原因。

A2 深入詳答

I've always hoped to work in the tourist industry. When I was thirteen, my parents gave me a booklet about North America that introduced the history of the national parks in the USA. I was totally impressed by the spectacular scenery and couldn't help wanting to discover more about the world. In addition, my parents are both tour guides and I have been deeply influenced by them. I also want to work in tourism so that I can help people appreciate all the beauty of the world.

我一直以來都想在旅遊業工作。我十三歲的時候，父母給了我一本有關北美的小冊子，內容介紹的是美國國家公園的歷史。當時我就對小冊子中的壯麗美景留下深刻的印象，忍不住想多了解這個世界。此外，我父母都是導遊，我深受他們的影響。我也想要在觀光業工作，如此我就可以協助人們欣賞這個世界的迷人之處。

Tips 面試一點通！

老闆想知道應徵者是受什麼樣的啟發，才因而對此領域產生熱忱。回答時，不要僅做像「我喜歡幫助別人」這類模糊的描述，應該要提出明確且讓人容易了解的實例。

Useful Expression 必通實用句型

[Someone] and [someone] are both working as [profession] and I am deeply influenced by them.

〔某人〕和〔某人〕都從事〔職業〕工作，我也深受其影響。

Power Vocabulary 好用字彙

influence [`ɪnfluəns] (v.) 影響
booklet [`buklɪt] (n.) 小冊子
spectacular [spɛk`tækjələ] (adj.) 壯觀的；驚人的
discover [dɪs`kʌvə] (v.) 發掘
beauty [`bjutɪ] (n.) 美麗

tourist [`turɪst] (adj.) 觀光的
impress [ɪm`prɛs] (v.) 使印象深刻
scenery [`sinərɪ] (n.) 景色
tourism [`turɪzəm] (n.) 觀光

✎ My own answer

Q 50

What is the most useful criticism you've received? What did you learn from it?

你受到過最有幫助的批評為何？你從當中學到什麼？

 **Track 51**

One of my previous managers said I was not an efficient and productive leader, because I underestimated the time needed to complete a project. I learned to examine tasks more carefully afterwards.

有一位前主管曾批評我不夠有效率，因為我低估了完成案子所需的時間。我後來學習到要更加仔細地評估分析案子。

A2 深入詳答

One of my previous managers once became upset with me since some projects I led were not being completed on time so our team lost some cases. He criticized me and pointed out that I was not an efficient and productive leader; our team lost some important clients because I underestimated the amount of time the projects would take us to complete. I thought the criticism was true and helpful and I learned it's important to examine tasks more carefully so I can better estimate the amount of time needed to complete them. In addition, I also need to build some flextime into projects in case something unexpected comes up.

有一位前主管曾因為我主導的一些計畫沒即時完成導致失掉一些案子而感到不太高興。他批評我並指出我不是個有效率和高產能的主管，因為我低估了完成案子所需要的時間，導致失去了一些客戶。我認為主管的批評並沒有錯，對我幫助很大。我學習到更謹慎地評估案子很重要，因為如此一來我才能更精確地估計結案需要的時間。另外，在執行案子的時候我也需要預留一些彈性時間，以應付突發狀況。

Tips 面試一點通！

這是個非常有意義的問題，人通常只喜歡聽好聽的話，對於別人的批評總是會否認或感到生氣。但是若能敞開心胸接受他人的意見，在經過仔細思考過後，通常會豁然開朗，有「對呀，我之前怎麼都沒想到過？」的醒悟。老闆想知道，面對批評時應徵者是否能虛心接受，又如何從中學習到自己不曾想過的事情。回答這個問題時，記得要以正面思考出發。

Useful Expression 必通實用句型

My manager criticized me and pointed out that I was not a [adjective] and [adjective] leader.

我的主管批評我並指出我不是一個〔形容詞〕和〔形容詞〕的領導者。

Power Vocabulary 好用字彙

previous [`prɪvɪs] (*adj.*) 之前的

examine [ɪg`zæmɪn] (*v.*) 檢查；細查

upset [ʌp`sɛt] (*adj.*) 沮喪的；苦惱的

point out 指出

underestimate [ˌʌndə`ɛstə.met] (*v.*) 低估

unexpected [ˌʌnɪk`spɛktɪd] (*adj.*) 無預期的

productive [prə`dʌktɪv] (*adj.*) 有收獲的；多產的

afterwards [`æftəwədz] (*adv.*) 之後；後來

criticize [`krɪtɪ.saɪz] (*v.*) 批評

efficient [ɪ`fɪʃənt] (*adj.*) 有效率的

flextime [`flɛks.taɪm] (*n.*) 彈性工作時間

✎ My own answer

Q51

Recently we've heard a lot about Customer Relationship Management, or CRM. Do you know what it is?

最近我們常聽到人們提到 "**CRM**" 一詞，你是否知道那是什麼？

 Track 52

A1 有力簡答

Basically, CRM is a process to ensure that a company establishes and maintains good relationships with customers. By working on customer relationships, companies are more likely to produce more profits.

基本上，CRM 是一個用來確認一家企業與客戶建立並維持良好關係的程序。透過跟客戶關係的建立，企業更有可能創造更高的獲利。

A2 深入詳答

Yes, I do hear a lot about CRM nowadays. To put it simply, CRM is the process of combining marketing, sales, and customer service within a company in order to ensure that customers are satisfied with our products and services. A company must maintain and enhance good relationships with customers in order to generate maximum profits. Let me provide you with an example. When I worked at BCC Software, all sales reps were required to work on customer relationships and thus could produce more revenues for the company. I think deploying CRM within a company can really give it a competitive advantage.

知道，我最近常聽到人們提到 CRM 一詞。簡單來說，CRM 是一個將公司內部的行銷、業務以及客戶服務整合在一起的程序，如此可確保客戶對我們的產品或服務感到滿意。一個公司必須跟客戶保持並加強良好的關係，以產生最大的獲利。讓我舉個例子。當我在 BCC 軟體公司工作的時候，所有的業務代表都被要求要照顧好客戶關係，以便能為公司創造更高的業績。我認為在公司內採用 CRM 確實可以增加公司的競爭優勢。

Tips 面試一點通！

此類題目會因專業領域不同，而有不一樣的問法。比方說，資訊產業老闆可能就會問「你知道 "Big Data"（海量資料）是什麼嗎？」這類關於該領域的 "Buzz word"（行話）。除了看履歷表上的經歷，老闆也想知道應徵者對產業新概念的吸收程度。因此，面試前可先多了解一下專業領域中是否有什麼新名詞或概念，事前準備一下，在面談時才可提供深入專業的回答。

Useful Expression 必通實用句型

A company must [do something] in order to generate maximum profits.

一個公司必須〔做某事〕以產生最高的獲利。

Power Vocabulary 好用字彙

process [ˋprɑsɛs] (n.) 程序；過程

maintain [menˋten] (v.) 維持

enhance [ɪnˋhæns] (v.) 提高；加強

deploy [dɪˋplɔɪ] (v.) 布署；展開；採用

ensure [ɪnˋʃur] (v.) 確保

combine [kəmˋbaɪn] (v.) 結合；綜合

generate [ˋdʒɛnə͵ret] (v.) 產生

competitive advantage 競爭優勢

My own answer

Q 52

Do you think advertising is the best way to promote a new product?

你是否認為廣告是推廣新產品的最佳方式？

A1 有力簡答 （以保養品業為例） **Track 53**

For some **FMCG** products advertising might work, but I think companies can **take advantage of** the Internet and promote new products in a more **cost-effective** manner.

廣告可能對一些消費性產品的推廣有幫助，但是我認為公司可以善加利用網際網路，並用更划算經濟的方式來推廣新產品。

A2 深入詳答

Well, it really depends on what kind of product we are talking about. If, for example, we were advertising a new facial cream, we might think that women reading a monthly fashion magazine might find it a more appropriate place to see an advertisement for a facial cream. Also we need to consider the size of the budget too, since you know, it is a major factor and some media might be way too expensive for us to use. Instead, I think some sort of promotional activities within the store, or to use some positive word-of-mouth to attract people's attention on the Internet will also be good ways to promote a new product.

嗯，這要視我們在講的是哪類產品而定。比方說，如果我們要幫一款新的臉部乳液做廣告，我們可能就會認為每個月閱讀時尚雜誌的女性可能會覺得雜誌就是乳液產品廣告該出現的地方。我們也得考慮預算的多寡，誠如您知道的，預算是個重要的因素，而且有些媒體對我們來說可能太昂貴以致我們無法採用。相反地，我倒認為在店內做促銷活動，或在網路上做正面的口碑行銷以吸引注意，都是推廣新產品的好方法。

Tips 面試一點通！

除了關於應徵者本身經驗或想法上的問題外，老闆也會想了解應徵者對專業
領域事物的看法。比如這道題目就是在問行銷相關的問題。這類問題或許沒
有標準答案，但不論應徵者提出的看法爲何，都一定要提出事實來佐證。如
本例，若應徵者認爲推廣產品不一定要靠廣告，就要進一步提出其他更好的
推廣方式。

Useful Expression 必通實用句型

**We need to consider [something] too, since it is a major factor.
[something] might be too expensive for us to use.**

我們也需考慮〔某事〕，因爲那是重要的一個因素。〔某事〕花費可能高到我們無法採用。

Power Vocabulary 好用字彙

FMCG 消費性產品（爲 Fast Moving Consuming Goods 簡稱）

take advantage of 利用

advertise [ˋædvəˌtaɪz] (*v.*) 登廣告

appropriate [əˋproprɪˌet] (*adj.*) 適當的

factor [ˋfæktə] (*n.*) 因素

word-of-mouth [ˋwɜdəvˋmauθ] (*n./adj.*) 口碑（的）；口耳相傳（的）

attract [əˋtrækt] (*v.*) 吸引

cost-effective [ˋkɔstəˋfɛktɪv] (*adj.*) 有成本效益的

facial cream 臉部乳液

budget [ˋbʌdʒɪt] (*n.*) 預算

media [ˋmidɪə] (*n.*) 媒體

promote [prəˋmot] (*v.*) 宣傳

✎ My own answer

Q 53 ▸

Tell me about when you have felt like giving up on a task.

請描述你曾想過放棄任務的情況。

A1 有力簡答 （以專案內容過於龐大為例） **Track 54**

Once, our team was working on a very large-scale project and it was so time-consuming that all members almost gave up. With help from our supervisor, we got the project done eventually.

有一次我們團隊負責執行一個非常大型的案子，因為太過耗時了，所有團員都幾乎想放棄。後來透過主管的協助，我們終於把案子完成了。

A2 深入詳答

Last year, I worked on a project where we had to make a 3-5 minute film to introduce the software company I worked for. My team came up with the idea of exploring software trends through the decades since we thought it would be exciting to see the innovations in software applications over the years. However, after actually working on it, we found that editing the film would be much more time-consuming than we had anticipated, especially when we tried to squeeze too much content into the film. So we almost wanted to give up on it. Eventually after our supervisor jumped in and mapped out a timeline, we could just concertrate on key elements and get the project done. The lesson I learned was to be realistic and focus on workable ideas only.

去年，我做過一個案子，我們必須製作一個三到五分鐘的影片介紹我服務的軟體公司。我們團隊想出了要探討十年來軟體趨勢的點子，因為我們覺得回顧過去軟體應用的各項創新會很有趣。但是當我們真正執行時才發現影片剪輯比我們預期的還花時間，尤其是當我們想將太多的內容擠到影片內的時候。所以大家幾乎想放棄不做了。最後我們的主管親自參與並替我們規劃好時間，我們才得以專注在重點上並將案子完成。由此我學到的教訓是要務實，並專注在可行的構想上。

Tips 面試一點通！

一般人聽到「放棄」兩字可能馬上就會有負面的聯想，但在現實的工作環境中，免不了會有一些事物是不值得投資時間在上面的。在這種狀況之下，與其埋頭苦幹，不如將時間做更佳的利用。要回答此題時不一定要說「我從沒想過放棄任務」，這樣聽起來有點刻意。直接回答曾有想放棄的經驗並無妨，不過當然要說明是經過一番努力和深思熟慮之後的決定，而不是連試都沒試，在一開頭就想放棄。

Useful Expression 必通實用句型

The lesson I learned was to be [adjective] and focus on [something] only.

由此我學到的教訓是要〔形容詞〕，並專注在〔某事〕上。

Power Vocabulary 好用字彙

scale [skel] (n.) 大小；規模

eventually [ɪˋvɛntʃʊəlɪ] (adv.) 終於

decade [ˋdɛked] (n.) 十年

application [͵æpləˋkeʃən] (n.) 應用；運用

squeeze [skwiz] (v.) 壓；擠

concentrate [ˋkɑnsɛn͵tret] (v.) 專注於……

realistic [rɪəˋlɪstɪk] (adj.) 切合實際的

time-consuming [ˋtaɪmkʌm͵sjumɪŋ] (adj.) 耗時的

explore [ɪkˋsplor] (v.) 探索

innovation [͵ɪnəˋveʃən] (n.) 創新

anticipate [ænˋtɪsə͵pet] (v.) 預期

map out 安排

element [ˋɛləmənt] (n.) 要素

workable [ˋwɝkəbl̩] (adj.) 切實可行的

✏ My own answer

Q54

What are the most important rewards you expect to gain from your career?

你最期待從工作中獲得什麼重要的回報？

A1 有力簡答 （以資訊科技工程師為例）

 Track 55

I always welcome challenges, so I'd like to get a sense of fulfillment by accomplishing difficult tasks.

我一直喜歡接受挑戰，所以我想從完成困難的任務中獲得成就感。

A2 深入詳答

I think a sense of self-fulfillment will be an important reward I can gain from my career. Furthermore, I always welcome challenges, so I expect to be challenged and keep improving myself. As an experienced IT engineer, I am confident that this senior position will allow me to advance further, and improve my knowledge of the IT industry. I expect to continue to grow and improve with the company.

我認為自我成就感就是我職涯中重要的回報。另外，我一直喜歡接受挑戰，因此我期待工作可帶給我足夠的挑戰，讓自己不斷進步。身為有經驗的資訊科技工程師，我有信心這個高級工程師職位可以讓我更精進，也可讓我學到更多的資訊科技產業的知識。我期待和公司一起不斷進步成長。

Tips 面試一點通！

多數應徵者一聽到 "rewards"（回報）就會直接想到薪水，的確，工作就是為了錢，但回答時目光應放遠一點，比如可以提到未來的發展性與自我成長等，讓老闆知道你是個重視自我成長且擁有長遠目標的人。

Useful Expression 必通實用句型

I always welcome challenges, so I expect to be challenged and keep improving myself.

我一直喜歡接受挑戰，因此我期待工作可帶給我足夠的挑戰，讓自己不斷進步。

Power Vocabulary 好用字彙

accomplish [ə`kɑmpəlɪʃ] (v.) 完成；實現

reward [rɪ`wɔrd] (n.) 報償；獎賞

career [kə`rɪr] (n.) 職涯

confident [`kɑnfədənt] (adj.) 有信心的；自信的

advance [əd`væns] (v.) 進展；進步

self-fulfillment [ˌsɛlffʊl`fɪlmənt] (n.) 自我實現

gain [gen] (v.) 獲得

IT 資訊科技（為 information technology 簡稱）

senior [`sinjə] (adj.) 資深的；較高階級的

continue [kən`tɪnju] (v.) 繼續

✎ My own answer

Q55

Why have you worked for so many companies in a short period of time?

你為什麼在短期內換過這麼多工作？

A1 有力簡答

 Track 56

I am always interested in learning, so I want to gain knowledge of different companies in the field. Now I am sure that my **accumulated** experience will enable me to **contribute** to your company goals.

我一直喜歡學習，所以我想從業界不同的公司吸取知識。現在，我很確定過去累積的經驗可讓我對貴公司的目標做出貢獻。

A2 深入詳答

Well, I am always interested in learning, so I want to gain knowledge of different companies in the field. Also when I just graduated from college two years ago, I was not really sure what job was a good fit for me. I was lucky to have opportunities to see how several different businesses operated. Now I have a pretty clear **understanding** of how your company operates, and to tell you the truth, I like the way your business works. I am confident that my previous experience will **enable** me to do well in your company.

我一直喜歡學習，所以我想從業界不同的公司吸收知識。另外，當我兩年前剛從大學畢業的時候，並不是很確定何種工作比較適合我。我很幸運有機會可以看到幾家不同的企業是如何運作的。現在我對貴公司的運作相當了解，老實說，我很喜歡貴公司的運作模式。我有信心之前的工作經驗可讓我在貴公司有所表現。

Tips 面試一點通！

只要老闆看履歷表的內容，馬上就可以推算出來，應徵者在多少時間內、做過幾個工作。若每個工作時間都很短（比方說只有幾個月或不滿一年）的話，老闆心裡就不免有所疑問。因此，若是常常換工作的應徵者，請務必好好準備一下此問題。

Useful Expression 必通實用句型

I was lucky to have opportunities to see how several different businesses operated.

我很幸運有機會可以看到幾家不同的企業是如何運作的。

Power Vocabulary 好用字彙

accumulate [əˈkjumjəˌlet] (v.) 累積
operate [ˈɑpəˌret] (v.) 運作；運轉
enable [ɪnˈebl] (v.) 使能夠

contribute [kənˈtrɪbjut] (v.) 貢獻
understanding [ˌʌndəˈstændɪŋ] (n.) 了解；認知

My own answer

Q 56

How would you describe empowerment? And how do you think employees can be empowered?

你如何看待「授權」？你認為員工應如何被授權？

A1 有力簡答

 Track 57

I think empowerment means that a boss encourages his workers to use their knowledge to overcome obstacles in the work environment. Workers should have the freedom to exercise their own judgement and make decisions.

我認為授權就是老闆鼓勵他的員工運用知識來克服工作上遇到的困難。員工應該要有展現判斷力和做決定的自由。

A2 深入詳答

From my point of view, empowerment is that feeling of responsibility and ownership that makes workers feel trusted. If I work with a boss who really lacks confidence to give employees responsibility, I probably won't be able to perform my best. Also I think a boss should empower workers by giving them the opportunity to decide the directional strategy of a task and then leave them to just go ahead and implement it. Of course, the boss should be in the background to support workers whenever they need assistance, but he or she should try not to always be breathing down their neck.

我的看法是，授權是責任和主導權的感覺，讓員工感覺到自己是受到信任的。如果我是和一個沒信心將責任交給員工的老闆共事，那我可能沒辦法發揮全部的潛力。另外，我認為老闆應該要能授權給員工，讓他們有機會決定任務的大方向策略，並放手讓他們去執行。當然，老闆也要在背後支持員工，在他們需要的時候提供協助，但是他或她不應老是在員工背後東窺西探。

Tips 面試一點通！

老闆不是三頭六臂，因此不可能將所有的事情都攬在自己身上，很多時候必須授權給員工去做決定。若老闆將權力抓得緊緊的，不放心把事情交給員工處理，對員工來說這並不是好事，因為員工可能會學不到東西。藉由此問老闆可以了解應徵者對授權的看法，以及是否準備好要接受老闆的授權。

I think a boss should empower workers by [doing something].
我認為老闆應該透過〔做某事〕授權給員工。

Power Vocabulary 好用字彙

empowerment [ɪmˋpaʊəmənt] (*n.*) 授權
obstable [ˋɑbstək!] (*n.*) 障礙
ownership [ˋonəˏʃɪp] (*n.*) 所有權
perform [pəˋfɔrm] (*v.*) 表現
strategy [ˋstrætədʒɪ] (*n.*) 策略
breathe down someone's neck 在某人背後東窺西探；緊盯某人

overcome [ˏovəˋkʌm] (*v.*) 克服；戰勝
responsibility [rɪˏspɑnsəˋbɪlətɪ] (*n.*) 責任
lack [læk] (*v.*) 缺乏
directional [dəˋrɛkʃən!] (*adj.*) 方向性的
assistance [əˋsɪstəns] (*n.*) 協助

🖊 **My own answer**

Q57

What is more important to you: the money (compensation package) or the work?

對你而言：金錢（薪資福利）和工作孰重？

 Track 58

A1 有力簡答

Although the salary is important, I still think whether I can enjoy the job and make a contribution to the company are far more important.

薪資固然重要，但我還是認為是否可以樂在工作並能為公司做出貢獻重要得多了。

A2 深入詳答

Well, I think salary is important since it is commensurate with my experience and abilities, but still it's just a piece of the package, not the only element. Many other elements go into making up a compensation package, such as the organizational culture, the challenges, and the room to advance. So I think what's more important is that I myself really enjoy the job, fit into the company environment, receive new challenges, and feel I am making a contribution to the company and thus work toward promotions in the future.

嗯，我認為薪資是重要的，因為它代表我的經驗和能力的等值回報，但那也只是整體報酬的一部分，並不是唯一要素。整體報酬還有很多其他的元素，像是企業文化、挑戰和升遷機會等。因此我認為更重要的是，我是否可以樂在工作、融入公司環境、接受新的挑戰並感受到自己為公司做出了貢獻，進而在將來獲得晉升機會。

Tips 面試一點通！

這是一道很重要且有深度的問題。由「職場新鮮人應該領 NTD 22K 還是 NTD19K？」這類新聞議題始終吵得火熱就可知道，人工作不外乎就是為了一份可以過活的薪水。但仔細想想，若工作真的全是為了賺錢餬口，無法自工作上學到任何東西，也就毫無成就感可言，日子肯定也不好過。因此，回答之道就是說兩者皆重要，並力求在二者之間取得平衡。

Useful Expression 必通實用句型

Salary is important since it is commensurate with my experience and abilities.

薪資是重要的，因為它代表我的經驗和能力付出的等值回報。

Power Vocabulary 好用字彙

contribution [ˌkɑntrəˋbjuʃən] (*n.*) 貢獻
element [ˋɛləmənt] (*n.*) 元素；要素
organizational culture 企業文化
promotion [prəˋmoʃən] (*n.*) 升遷

commensurate [kəˋmɛnʃərɪt] (*adj.*) 同量的；等值的
compensation [ˌkɑmpənˋseʃən] (*n.*) 報酬；薪償
environment [ɪnˋvaɪrənmənt] (*n.*) 環境

✎ My own answer

Q 58

What specific goals have you set for your career?

你對自己的職涯設立什麼樣的目標？

I want to work at a **prestigious** company where I can **apply** what I have learned. And my long-term goal is to start my own business.

我想要在一家有名望的公司學以致用。我長期的目標則是開創自己的公司。

A2 深入詳答

In the mean time, I am trying hard to get myself well-prepared for the **technical** support engineer position. And then I want to be working for a prestigious company in a job in which I can **contribute** my technical support skills. Assisting customers with their computer problems and providing them with **workable** solutions really give me a **sense of accomplishment.** So my long-term career goal is to be the best computer **technician** I can for the company I work for, and hope to **establish** my own technical **firm** one day.

目前，我正在努力充實自己以便能勝任技術支援工程師的職位。接下來我想要進入一家有名望的公司以貢獻我在技術支援方面的能力。協助客戶處理電腦問題並提供可行的解決方案確實讓我很有成就感。因此，我長期的職涯目標就是努力成為公司的最佳電腦技術人員，也期望有一天可以開創自己的技術公司。

Tips 面試一點通！

既然是問職涯的目標，那就要宏觀一些。回答時應做較長遠、大方向的目標設定，而非只談眼前的近利。

Useful Expression 必通實用句型

My long-term career goal is to be a [someone].

我的長期職涯目標是成為一個〔某（樣的）人〕。

Power Vocabulary 好用字彙

prestigious [prɛsˋtɪdʒɪəs] (*adj.*) 有名望的
technical [ˋtɛknɪkl] (*adj.*) 技術上的
workable [ˋwɜkəbl] (*adj.*) 切實可行的
technician [tɛkˋnɪʃən] (*n.*) 技術人員
firm [fɜm] (*n.*) 公司；行號

apply [əˋplaɪ] (*v.*) 應用
contribute [kənˋtrɪbjut] (*v.*) 貢獻
sense of accomplishment 成就感
establish [əˋstæblɪʃ] (*v.*) 創立；建立

✎ My own answer

I see from your CV that you worked at ABC non-profit organization. How was that experience?

我在履歷表上看到你曾在 ABC 非營利組織工作過。那是什麼樣的經驗？

A1 有力簡答　（以兒童福利機構為例）　 Track 60

That was a valuable experience for me since I helped to protect children and develop their potential. I myself also learned a lot from the job.

那對我來說是個很寶貴的經驗，因為我協助保護兒童並開發他們的潛力。我自己也從中學到很多。

A2 深入詳答

I was in charge of media and marketing so my job was really to promote our organization. I enjoyed it fundamentally because I was doing something I had passion for. For me, a job must be about more than just making money. So, when I worked there, I was helping to protect children and develop their potential, which I enjoyed a lot. It was also an interesting job to work with the media. That job actually helped me to learn and develop as a person every day.

我負責的是媒體和行銷，所以我的工作就是推展我們的組織。我打從心底喜歡那份工作，因為對於我所做的事我具有相當的熱情。對我來說，工作不應只是為了賺錢，因此當我在那裡工作時，我協助保護兒童並開發他們的潛能，而我做得非常開心。另外，跟媒體互動也很有趣。那個工作確實讓我每天都有機會學習並發展自我。

Tips 面試一點通！

面試官在問的是某公司的實際經驗，當然老闆也會想了解某個特定公司的營運情形。因此，不要只提一般性的日常事務，而要應針對該單位或公司的強項以及自己所扮演的角色做進一步說明。

Useful Expression 必通實用句型

I was in charge of [task]. I enjoyed it fundamentally because I was doing something I had passion for.

我負責的是〔任務〕。我打從心底喜歡那份工作，因為對於我所做的事我具有相當的熱情。

Power Vocabulary 好用字彙

valuable [ˋvæljuəbl] (*adj.*) 寶貴的

potential [pəˋtɛnʃəl] (*n.*) 潛力；潛能

fundamentally [ˌfʌndəˋmɛntḷɪ] (*adj.*) 根本地；本質地

protect [prəˋtɛkt] (*v.*) 保護

promote [prəˋmot] (*v.*) 推廣；行銷

passion [ˋpæʃən] (*n.*) 熱情

✎ My own answer

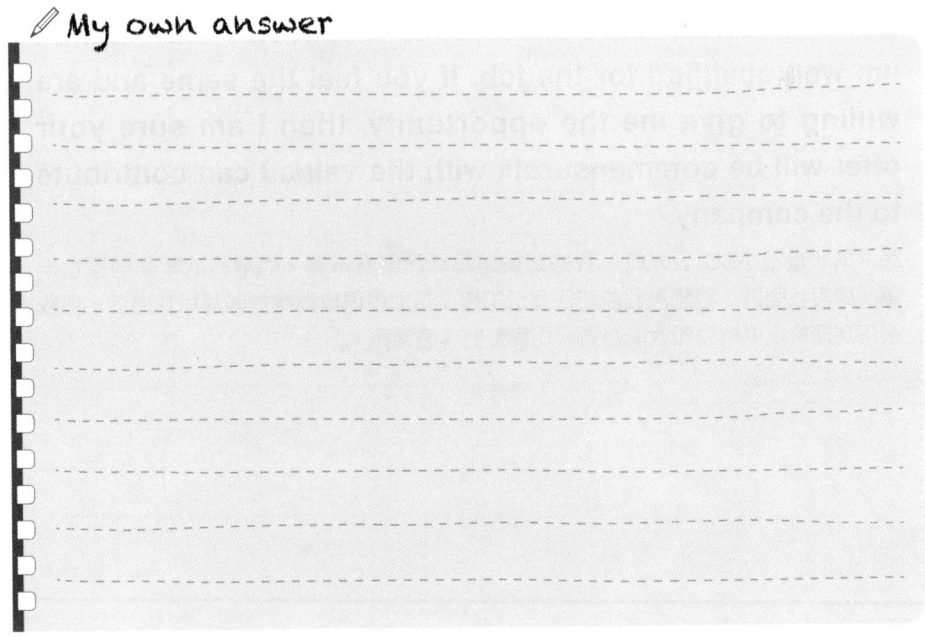

Q60

What are your starting and final levels of compensation?

你最初和後來的薪資水準為何？

A1 有力簡答

 **Track 61**

In ABC Company, my annual salary started at NT$500K two years ago and the final level of my salary was NT$700K.

兩年前在 ABC 公司時，我的起薪是每年新台幣五十萬，而最終的年薪則達七十萬。

A2 深入詳答

Well, in ABC Company, my annual salary started at NT$500K two years ago and the final level of my salary was NT$700K. Please allow me to emphasize that I think I am well qualified for the job. If you feel the same and are willing to give me the opportunity, then I am sure your offer will be commensurate with the value I can contribute to the company.

嗯，兩年前在 ABC 公司時，我的起薪是每年台幣五十萬，而最終的年薪則達七十萬。請容我強調，我認為我能勝任此份工作。若您也這樣認為並願意給我機會，那我很確定您會提供給我和我能為貴公司貢獻的等值報酬。

Tips 面試一點通！

面談到最後，若公司和應徵者都認為彼此可合作，當然就會討論到薪資問題。老闆之所以會問應徵者上一份工作的薪資是多少，是因為他或她想了解應徵者在市場上的行情如何，並以此為參考，看該提供應徵者多少薪資才合理。因此，照實回答無妨，不要試圖亂加數字，因為如果老闆日後向前任公司尋求 reference（查核）而發現應徵者所言與事實不符，那麼應徵者的信用便會被打折扣。

Useful Expression 必通實用句型

In [company name], my annual salary started at [amount] and the final level of my salary was [amount].

在〔公司名稱〕，我的起薪是每年〔金額〕，而最終的年薪則達〔金額〕。

Power Vocabulary 好用字彙

annual salary 年薪
emphasize [ˋɛmfəˌsaɪz] (v.) 強調
qualified [ˋkwɑləˌfaɪd] (adj.) 合格的；勝任的
commensurate [kəˋmɛnʃərɪt] (adj.) 等量的；相稱的
value [ˋvæljʊ] (n.) 價值

✎ My own answer

 **精選好用句型，一次入袋！**

　　學完本單元的高頻問題及擬答後，試著寫下自己的答案，最後再複習一次本單元的好用句型，有助於在面試時靈活套用，秀出最好的一面！

▶ 說明對加班的看法

☐ **I do understand the importance of meeting deadlines and getting jobs done on time. So when the situation requires I take work home, it's not a problem for me.**
我的確了解在截止期限前將工作做完的重要性。因此，如果情況需要我將工作帶回家做，我沒問題。

▶ 說明之前工作的顯著成就

☐ **I help [company name] regain good reputation and boost [company's] sales revenue by [amount].**
我協助〔公司名稱〕重獲好名聲，並大幅增加了〔公司〕的營收達〔數字〕。

▶ 說明前任公司的競爭優勢

☐ **When we develop our business strategies, we focus on [something] and [something] we could offer.**
當我們在發展商業策略時，我們將重點放在我們提供〔某事〕和〔某事〕上。

▶ 說明解決問題的程序

☐ **I try to identify the problem and possible factors first, then investgate causes and work on solutions to the problem.**
我會先試著找出問題點和導致問題的可能因素，然後調查問題的起因並找出問題的解決方案。

▶ 說明前份工作的職務內容

☐ **I was in charge of [something]. My duties included [doing something], [doing something], and [doing something].**
我主要負責〔某事〕。我的責任範圍包括〔做某事〕、〔做某事〕和〔做某事〕。

▶ 說明與前任主管的相處情形

☐ **It was a valuable experience working for my previous supervisor, [name]. He [do something], [do something], and [do something] in a** very professional manner.

我跟前主管〔人名〕共事的經驗是很珍貴的。他在〔做某事〕、〔做某事〕及〔做某事〕上都很專業。

▶ 說明化解衝突方式

☐ In order to resolve the conflict, I try to be direct, clarify what is going on, and proactively work with others to reach a proper resolution.

為了化解衝突，我會試著表明態度、弄清楚狀況，並主動和其他人合作共同找出適當的解決之道。

▶ 說明進入工作領域或行業的原因

☐ [Someone] and [Someone] are both working as [profession] and I am deeply influenced by them.

〔某人〕和〔某人〕都從事〔職業〕工作，我也深受其影響。

▶ 說明從某件事學到的教訓

☐ The lesson I learned was to be [adjective] and focus on [something] only.

由此我學到的教訓是要〔形容詞〕，並專注在〔某事〕上。

▶ 說明換工作的原因

☐ I always welcome challenges, so I expect to be challenged and keep improving myself.

我一直喜歡面對挑戰，因此我期待工作可帶給我足夠的挑戰，讓自己不斷進步。

▶ 說明短期內頻繁換工作的原因

☐ I was lucky to have opportunities to see how several different businesses operated.

我很幸運有機會可以看到幾個不同的企業是如何運作的。

▶ 說明前份工作的薪資範圍

☐ In [company name], my annual salary started at [amount] and the final level of my salary was [amount].

在〔公司名稱〕，我的起薪是每年〔金額〕，而最終的年薪則達〔金額〕。

NOTES

Part 4
關於未來工作的問題：發展／期望

Questions about the Future:

Professional Development / Expectations

Q61

What do you know about our organization?
你對我們公司認識多少？

A1 有力簡答 （以系統服務公司為例）

 **Track 62**

Learning from news releases and your company website, I know you are a respected international company specializing in providing IT services to large enterprise clients around the world.

從新聞報導和貴公司的網站，我得知貴公司是一家受敬重的國際性公司，專門提供資訊科技服務給全球的大型企業客戶。

A2 深入詳答

Learning from some recent news releases, I know you are a large and respected international company. You mainly provide IT services to large enterprise clients and government agencies around the world. Over the last 12 years, your company has demonstrated the ability to develop practical IT solutions and tools to help clients increase productivity, profitability, and competitiveness. In reviewing your company website, I've also familiarized myself with your company mission and objectives.

從最近的新聞報導，我得知貴公司是一家大型且受敬重的國際性公司。貴公司主要提供資訊科技服務給全球的大型企業客戶和政府單位。過去十二年間，貴公司展現了開發實際可行的資訊科技解決方案與工具的能力，協助客戶增加生產力、獲利能力與競爭優勢。在審視過貴公司的網站後，我也對貴公司的使命和目標有了更深的認識。

如同之前提到的，面談前務必將目標公司的背景、產品、組織和客戶群等做好充分研究。（相關的資訊可由網路或新聞報導等來源蒐集得知。）

Useful Expression 必通實用句型

In reviewing your company [something], I've familiarized myself with your company mission and objectives.
在審視過貴公司的〔某事物〕後，我對貴公司的使命和目標有了更深的認識。

Power Vocabulary 好用字彙

news release 新聞的發布
enterprise [ˋɛntɚˌpraɪz] (*n.*) 企業
practical [ˋpræktɪkl̩] (*adj.*) 實際的
profitability [ˌprɑfɪtəˋbɪlətɪ] (*n.*) 獲利力
familiarize [fəˋmɪljəˌraɪz] (*v.*) 使熟悉
objective [əbˋdʒɛktɪv] (*n.*) 目標

respected [rɪˋspɛktɪd] (*adj.*) 受敬重的
demonstrate [ˋdɛmənˌstret] (*v.*) 展示；證明
productivity [ˌprɑdʌkˋtɪvətɪ] (*n.*) 生產力
competitiveness [kəmˋpɛtətɪvnɪs] (*n.*) 競爭優勢
mission [ˋmɪʃən] (*n.*) 使命

✎ My own answer

Q62

What kinds of problems do you enjoy solving?

你喜歡處理哪一類問題？

 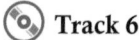 **Track 63**

I am good at dealing with software programming problems. I enjoy the process of analyzing the information, diagnosing the problem, and coming up with a solution.

我擅長處理軟體程式的問題。我很喜歡分析資訊、找出問題並想出解決方案的過程。

A2 深入詳答

Well, I find this question interesting because as a software developer I don't feel satisfied with my work unless I really solve some program related or coding problems. I enjoy the process of analyzing the information, diagnosing the coding problem, and eventually coming up with a proper solution. When I worked at TOP Software Company, whenever other software programmers had trouble with program coding, they turned to me for assistance. I enjoy the feeling of being the creative mind behind software applications.

嗯，我覺得這個問題很有趣，因為身為一個軟體開發人員，除非可以真正解決程式相關或寫程式的問題，否則我不會對我的工作感到滿足。我很喜歡分析資訊、找出程式問題並在最後想出適當的解決方案的過程。當我在 TOP 軟體公司工作時，只要其他軟體開發人員編寫程式遇到困難，他們都會尋求我的協助。我很喜歡身為軟體應用程式背後那個創意人的那種感覺。

Tips 面試一點通！

先前提過，老闆會重視員工是否有「解決問題的能力」(problem-solving skills)。當然，職場上會發生的問題有些關係到產品，有些則是關於人際溝通或員工互動的問題。回應時，端視應徵者擅長處理哪一類的問題，只須據實際的狀況回答即可。

Useful Expression 必通實用句型

I enjoy the process of [doing someting], [doing something], and eventually coming up with a proper solution.

我很喜歡〔做某事〕、〔做某事〕並在最後想出適當的解決方案的過程。

Power Vocabulary 好用字彙

good at 擅長

diagnose [ˋdaɪəgnoz] (v.) 診斷

software developer 軟體開發人員

unless [ʌnˋlɛs] (prep.) 除非

proper [ˋprɑpə] (adj.) 恰當的；適合的

creative [krɪˋetɪv] (adj.) 有創意的

analyze [ˋænlˌaɪz] (v.) 分析

come up with （針對問題）想出

satisfied [ˋsætɪsˌfaɪd] (adj.) 滿足的

code [kod] (v.) 編寫程式

assistance [əˋsɪstəns] (n.) 協助

application [ˌæpləˋkeʃən] (n.) 應用程式

✎ My own answer

Q63 ▶

What plans do you have for continued study?

你打算如何繼續進修？

A1 有力簡答　（以電腦技術為例）

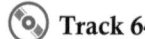 **Track 64**

I plan to obtain the latest knowledge by taking courses, attending conferences, and listening to webinars on the Internet.

我計畫經由上課、參加討論會，和收聽網路研討會來取得最新的知識。

A2 深入詳答

Oh, yes, of course I have plans to keep learning updated knowledge. Although I have obtained my master degree in Computer Science, my previous administrator encouraged me to expand my knowledge base and stay up-to-date on new developments. New technologies today may become obsolete in two or three years. So I plan to learn the latest information by taking university coursework, or attending new technology related conferences and seminars. In addition, taking online courses may also be a good alternative for a busy technician like me.

噢，是的，我當然有計畫要不斷學習新知。雖然我已經有電腦碩士學位，我之前的主管還是鼓勵我要拓展自己的知識，了解最新的發展。今日的新科技可能過兩、三年就會被淘汰，因此，我計畫要透過選修大學的課程，或參加新技術相關的討論會和研討會來學習最新知識。除此之外，對像我這種忙碌的技術人員來說，選修一些線上課程也是個不錯的選擇。

Tips 面試一點通！

所謂「活到老，學到老」，老闆提此問題就是想聽聽應徵者是否有不斷學習的心。因此，即便已有深厚的知識和技術，最好還是要有不斷追求新知、充實自我的精神。

Useful Expression 必通實用句型

I plan to obtain the latest knowledge by [doing A], [doing B], and [doing C].

我計畫經由〔做 A〕，〔做 B〕，和〔做 C〕方式來習得最新的知識。

Power Vocabulary 好用字彙

obtain [əb`ten] (*v.*) 取得

conference [`kɑnfərəns] (*n.*) 正式會議；討論會

webinar [`wɛbəˌnɑr] (*n.*) 網路研討會（由 web 和 seminar 組成）

updated [ʌp`det] (*adj.*) 更新的；最新的

administrator [əd`mɪnəˌstretə] (*n.*) 管理者；治理者

encourage [ɪn`kɝɪdʒ] (*v.*) 鼓勵

up-to-date [`ʌptə`det] (*adj.*) 最新的；包含最新資訊的

obsolete [`ɑbsəˌlit] (*adj.*) 汰舊的；廢棄的

alternative [ɔl`tɝnətɪv] (*n.*) 其他的選擇

✎ My own answer

Q 64 >

What do you see yourself doing in five years?

你認為五年後你的事業狀況會是什麼樣子？

 **Track 65**

In five years, I would like to be a customer service manager leading my team to provide satisfactory services to customers.

五年後，我想成為客服經理，帶領自己的團隊提供客戶滿意的服務。

A2 深入詳答

I thought about that the other day too. I still see myself in customer service in five years. I hope that I will have developed the competencies and sufficient experience to be considered for a leadership position in customer service, either as a manager or assistant manager. I would like to lead a team, say, with a staff of five and provide customers with good and satisfactory service. In order to achieve that, I want to continually improve my interpersonal and communication skills. This is what I've always loved to do.

前兩天我自己也思考到這個問題。我認為五年後我還是會在客戶服務的領域。我希望到時我已具備足以領導客服部門的能力與經驗，擔任經理或副理。我想要自己帶一個團隊，比方說一個五人團隊，提供優質、令人滿意的服務給客戶。為了達成此目標，我要持續地精進我在人際關係與溝通方面的技巧。這是我一直以來喜愛做的事。

Tips 面試一點通！

老闆想透過此問題來了解應徵者的中期目標，因此應避免提供短視的答案，而應將焦點放在自己的強項上，並說明在未來五年中會如何善用自己的強項來達成目標。

Useful Expression 必通實用句型

I hope that I will have developed the competencies and experience to be considered for a [position].

我希望我已具備可以勝任〔職位〕的能力和經驗。

Power Vocabulary 好用字彙

satisfactory [ˌsætɪsˈfæktərɪ] (adj.) 令人滿意的；符合要求的
competency [ˈkɑmpətənsɪ] (n.) 能力；勝任
sufficient [səˈfɪʃənt] (adj.) 足夠的
leadership [ˈlidəʃɪp] (n.) 領導地位；統御力
achieve [əˈtʃiv] (v.) 達成
continually [kənˈtɪnjʊəlɪ] (adv.) 持續地
interpersonal [ˌɪntəˈpɜsənḷ] (adj.) 人際的；人與人之間的

✎ My own answer

If hired, when can you start work?

如果被錄取了，你何時可以上班？

 Track 66

A1 有力簡答

While I would like to start work as soon as possible, please allow about two weeks to transfer my responsibilities to colleagues at my current employer.

雖然我想儘早開始上班，但還是請給我大約兩週時間，讓我可以把目前在公司負責的工作交接給其他同事。

A2 深入詳答

I am really interested in this position, and will be eager to start work as soon as possible. But the issue is that I probably need some time, say, one week to two weeks, to transfer my responsibilities to other coworkers at my current employer. In addition, I am willing to use these two weeks to study your products in advance and officially start work in two weeks.

我對於這個職缺很有興趣，非常希望可以儘早開始上班。但是問題是，我可能需要一些時間，比方一個或兩個禮拜，好將我目前在公司負責的工作交接給公司的其他同事。除此之外，我願意利用這兩個禮拜的時間事先研究一下貴公司的產品，兩個禮拜之後正式開始上班。

Tips 面試一點通！

這道題目在面談時幾乎是所有老闆必問的問題。老闆會想了解應徵者的時間
安排，看應徵者是否可以銜接上公司內部的人事規劃。比方說，公司某位員
工可能三月中要離職，老闆可能希望找來的新人在三月中就能來交接。建議
可先讓對方感受到你對這份工作的高度意願，再依照個人狀況誠實回答可到
職的時間即可。

Useful Expression 必通實用句型

**Please allow about [number of days] to transfer my responsibilities
to colleagues at my current employer.**

請給我大約〔天數〕的時間，讓我可以把目前在公司負責的工作交接給其他同事。

Power Vocabulary 好用字彙

transfer [træns`fɝ] (*v.*) 轉移；交接

colleague [`kɑlig] (*n.*) 同事；同僚

in advance 事先

responsibility [rɪˌspɑnsə`bɪlətɪ] (*n.*) 責任

current [`kɝənt] (*adj.*) 目前的；現在的

officially [ə`fɪʃəlɪ] (*adv.*) 正式地

✐ My own answer

Q66

Are you willing to put the interests of the company ahead of your own?

你是否願意把公司利益擺在個人利益之前？

A1 有力簡答

🔊 Track 67

If the situation requires it, I am willing to work on weekends in order to get my work done. But I definitely don't want to lie to customers in order to make a sale.

若情況需要，我願意為了完成份內的工作而在週末加班。但是我當然不想為了做到生意而對客戶說謊。

A2 深入詳答

That's a question worth considering. Please give me a second to organize my thoughts. Well, I would say it really depends. If it's a situation that a project deadline is approaching and all team members are required to work on weekends, I am willing to do so even if it means I have to sacrifice my own spare time. However, I certainly don't want to lie to customers in order to close a deal. So, I think it really depends on different situations.

這是個值得思考的問題。請給我一點時間組織一下我的想法。嗯，我會說這要視狀況而定。如果是案子期限就快到了，所有團隊成員都必須在週末加班，那我會願意這樣做，即便那意味著我必須犧牲個人的空閒時間。不過，若只是為了結案而對客戶說謊，那我當然不願意了。所以，我認為真的要視不同狀況而定。

Tips 面試一點通！

這是一個頗難回答的問題。若說一定會先考慮公司利益，聽起來過於矯情，但若是一切以個人利益為優先，又似乎不符合公司的期待。因此，最好是折衷的回應，比方說你會視狀況而定，或者說你認為應以客戶的利益為優先考量等。

Useful Expression 必通實用句型

I am willing to work on weekends even if it means I have to sacrifice my own spare time.

我願意在週末加班，即便那意味著我必須犧牲個人的空閒時間。

Power Vocabulary 好用字彙

organize [ˋɔrɡəˌnaɪz] (v.) 組織
deadline [ˋdɛdˌlaɪn] (n.) 期限
sacrifice [ˋsækrəˌfaɪs] (v.) 犧牲
certainly [ˋsɝtənlɪ] (adv.) 必定地；當然

thought [θɔt] (n.) 想法
approach [əˋprotʃ] (v.) 接近
spare time 空閒時間

✎ My own answer

Q 67

What short-term objectives have you established for yourself?

你為自己設的短期目標為何？

A1 有力簡答　（以專案管理人員為例）　　　 **Track 68**

My short-term goals are to achieve my PMP certification and to score at least 900 on the TOEIC test within two months.

我的短期目標是在兩個月內獲得 PMP 證照，並在多益檢定考試中拿到至少九百分的成績。

A2 深入詳答

My short-term objectives are to earn my PMP certification within these two months and to score at least 900 on the TOEIC test. I've been preparing for these two tests for quite a long time. Of course, in addition to studying PMP theory, it would be beneficial for me to apply knowledge acquired from the books to a real-world situation. And I always want to score higher on TOEIC, so I plan to take the test once again next month.

我的短期目標是在兩個月得到 PMP 認證，PMP 指的是「專案管理人員」，我也想在多益測驗中拿到至少 900 分的成績。我已經花了很多時間準備這兩項考試。當然，除了學習 PMP 專案管理的理論之外，若能將書本上學習到的知識應用在真實的情況，對我將會很有助益。而我一直希望能夠在多益測驗有更好的成績，所以我計畫下個月再參加一次考試。

Tips 面試一點通！

做任何事情一定要有目標。老闆會想了解應徵者的短期目標爲何，也就是近期內可做到或可達成的事項，比方說，學會某種語言或電腦課程進修等。

Useful Expression 必通實用句型

My short-term objectives are to [do something] and [do something] within [time period].

我短期內的目標是在〔期限〕以內〔做某事〕和〔做某事〕。

Power Vocabulary 好用字彙

short-term [`ʃɔrt`tɝm] (adj.) 短期的
PMP 專案管理人員（為 Project Management Professional 的簡稱）
certification [ˌsɝtɪfəˈkeʃən] (n.) 認證；檢定
score [skor] (v.) 得分
objective [əbˈdʒɛktɪv] (n.) 目標
theory [ˈθiərɪ] (n.) 理論
beneficial [ˌbɛnəˈfɪʃəl] (adj.) 有利的；有好處的

✎ My own answer

Q68

How do you plan to achieve these objectives?
你打算怎麼做才能達成這些目標？

A1 有力簡答 （承上題，以專案管理人員為例） 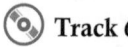 Track 69

Besides the training courses I am currently taking, I would like to obtain real hands-on experience by managing projects in the company.

除了我目前在上的訓練課程之外，我也想藉由在公司管理專案獲得實務經驗。

A2 深入詳答

Well, as you may know already, managers who want to get PMP certification must demonstrate a solid foundation of project management experience and competency. So besides the PMP training courses I am currently taking, I would like to obtain real hands-on experience by managing projects in the company. That way, not only can I apply my project management knowledge to real business situations, but the company can also benefit from my professional contributions.

嗯，誠如您可能已經知道的，想取得 PMP 認證的經理人員，必須能夠展現出扎實的專案管理經驗與能力。所以，除了現在正在上的 PMP 訓練課程，我希望能夠在公司內管理專案以獲得真正的實務經驗。這樣一來，我不僅可將自己的專案管理知識應用在實際的商務情境中，公司也可以從我專業貢獻中獲益。

Tips 面試一點通！

承上題，在目標設定好之後就是要有行動的步驟了。比方說，若想學好英語，你可以參加英語會話班、閱讀英文文章，或是參加英文讀書會等。總之，記得要說出具體的行動，才有說服力。

Useful Expression 必通實用句型

Besides the [course name] I am taking, I would also like to obtain real hands-on experience by [doing something].

除了我目前在上的〔課程名稱〕外，我也想藉由〔做某事〕獲得實務經驗。

Power Vocabulary 好用字彙

demonstrate [ˋdɛmənˌstret] (v.) 展示；證明
solid [ˋsɑlɪd] (adj.) 扎實的
foundation [faʊnˋdeʃən] (n.) 基礎
competency [ˋkɑmpətənsɪ] (n.) 能力 (= competence)
obtain [əbˋten] (v.) 取得；獲得
hands-on experience 實際執行的經驗

✐ My own answer

Q69

What interests you about this job?
這份工作讓你感興趣的部分為何？

A1 有力簡答 （以飲料產品品牌經理為例） **Track 70**

I am interested in this position because it allows me to make use of my experience. And I also see a lot of room for me to advance in your company.

我對這個職缺有興趣，因為這個職位讓我有機會應用我的經驗，另外，我也看到在貴公司有許多讓我可以獲得升遷的空間。

A2 深入詳答

Well, I am interested in this beverage brand manager position, not only because it allows me to make best use of my experience and skills, but I also think there will be a lot of room for me to advance in your company. I am good at developing marketing strategies for beverage products, and I want to apply my skills to benefit your company. And I am sure this position will also offer me opportunities to enrich my experience. So I can grow with the company.

嗯，我之所以對於這個飲料品牌經理的工作非常有興趣，不僅是因為這份工作可以讓我發揮我的經驗與技能，而且我認為在貴公司有許多讓我可以獲得升遷的空間。我擅長為飲料產品擬定行銷策略，我希望能運用我的技能來幫助貴公司。我也非常確定這個工作可以提供我機會，讓我的經驗更加豐富，這樣我就可以與公司一起成長。

Tips 面試一點通！

一般而言，應徵者應該是對徵才廣告上的某個工作內容感興趣，才會寄出履歷申請工作。那麼回答這題，就將自己對工作感興趣的部分提出討論即可。記得，回答時不要只繞著自己的興趣或期望打轉，而應從如何能幫助未來公司獲利或改善某類問題等角度切入。

Useful Expression 必通實用句型

I am good at [doing something], and I want to apply my skills to benefit your company.

我擅長〔做某事〕，我希望能運用我的技能來幫助公司。

Power Vocabulary 好用字彙

room (for someone) to advance（某人）有升遷的空間

beverage [ˈbɛvərɪdʒ] (n.) 飲料

be good at 擅長於

benefit [ˈbɛnɪfɪt] (v.) 有益於

enrich [ɪnˈrɪtʃ] (v.) 使豐富

My own answer

Q70

What challenges are you looking for in this position?

你預期此份工作會面臨到的挑戰為何？

Well, one new challenge for me is to promote products in other markets **overseas**. I welcome this new challenge and I will do my best to do more research into international markets.

嗯，對我來說，在海外市場推廣產品會是一項新挑戰。我很期待這個新挑戰，也會盡全力針對國際市場多做些研究。

A2 深入詳答

I studied **business administration** in college and worked as an assistant maketing **specialist** at Good-Lab Company. I have experience of product marketing in Taiwan **domestically**. Before doing any **promotion**, I had to know our facial cream products, our **competitors**, and our **target markets**. Now in this postion, I would say that to **market** products overseas is **challenging** for me. But I welcome this challenge, I mean, I consider that international marketing strategy is about **extending** the **techniques** used in the domestic market, right? So at the same time, it's a great opportunity for me to do more research into the international markets.

我在學校學的是企業管理，並曾在 Good-Lab 公司擔任助理行銷專員。我有在台灣負責產品行銷的經驗。在進行任何促銷活動之前，我必須知道我們的面霜產品、競爭對手與目標市場。就現今這個職缺來看，我想行銷產品到海外對我來說是個挑戰。但是我很期待這樣的挑戰，我的意思是，我認為國際行銷策略是一種國內行銷技術的延伸，不是嗎？ 所以同時，這對我來說是很好的機會，讓我能針對國際市場多做些研究。

Tips 面試一點通！

在工作上的挑戰無可避免，但可以先預期會有的問題，事先採取行動以減少可能帶來的衝擊。老闆藉由此題目來判斷應徵者對工作的了解程度，以及會用什麼方式讓自己更快進入狀況。回答時不要只談挑戰本身，還要提到自己可以針對挑戰做些什麼。比方說，新工作可能必須會使用某個會計軟體，但之前沒接觸過可能會是個困難，提出自己願意在下班時間去上電腦課程，以便於短期內快速上手，就會是不錯的回應。

Useful Expression 必通實用句型

I would say that to [do something] is challenging for me, but I welcome this challenge.

我會說〔做某事〕對我來說會頗具挑戰性，但我頗期待這個新挑戰。

Power Vocabulary 好用字彙

overseas [`ovəsiz] (adj./ adv.) 海外的／在海外
specialist [`spɛʃəlɪst] (n.) 專員；專家
promotion [prə`moʃən] (n.) 推廣；促銷
target market 目標市場
challenging [`tʃælɪndʒɪŋ] (adj.) 具挑戰性的
technique [tɛk`nik] (n.) 技巧

business administration 企業管理
domestically [də`mɛstɪklɪ] (adv.) 國內地
competitor [kəm`pɛtətə] (n.) 競爭者；對手
market [`mɑrkɪt] (v.) （在市場上）銷售
extend [ɪk`stɛnd] (v.) 延伸

✎ My own answer

Q71

Do you think you should be more like others, or do you think you should be different from everyone else in order to succeed?

你認為要成功的話，你應該和其他人一樣，還是要與眾不同？

A1 有力簡答

 Track 72

I think a person should try to differentiate himself from others and bring his unique talents to the table in order to be outstanding and successful.

我認為要出眾、成功，一個人應該要試著讓自己與眾不同，並貢獻自己的特殊才能。

A2 深入詳答

This question leads me to think of my marketing team at Chaiix Taiwan. All the individuals in the team are exceptionally talented, but of course, have different skills. Based on my own experience, I certainly don't think a person should be more like others in order to succeed. Instead, an individual should try to differentiate himself from others and bring his unique talents to the table. I know in Taiwan, people tend to be more conservative. But if a person keeps worrying that his ideas may be too wild and might not be acceptable to others, then he is more likely to miss out on a lot of opportunities to succeed.

這個問題讓我想到我在台灣 Chaiix 公司的行銷團隊。團隊裡每個人都是才華獨具，不過當然是每個人擁有不一樣的技能。基於我個人的經驗，我當然不認為一個人應該和其他人一樣才能夠成功。相反地，他應該要想辦法與眾不同，並貢獻其獨特的天賦。我知道在台灣多數的人都比較保守。但是如果一個人一直擔心自己的想法很奇怪，也許不會被別人接受，那他很可能會因此而錯失許多成功的機會。

Tips 面試一點通！

在現在競爭激烈的市場環境中，企業面臨到產品、服務等同質性問題的機會越來越高，要如何創新找到企業的藍海策略，是一大挑戰。老闆想要藉由此問題，進一步了解應徵者是否只想要一份工作，做個一般的上班族，還是喜歡與眾不同，有創新和追求差異性的精神。喜歡追求創新的人比較有機會爲公司注入新氣象和新構想。

Useful Expression 必通實用句型

I don't think a person should [do something] in order to succeed. Instead, an individual should try to [do something].

我不認為一個人應該〔做某事〕才能成功。相反地，他應該想辦法〔做某事〕。

Power Vocabulary 好用字彙

differentiate [ˌdɪfəˋrɛnʃɪˌet] (*v.*) 差異化
outstanding [ˋaʊtˋstændɪŋ] (*adj.*) 出衆的
exceptionally [ɪkˋsɛpʃənəlɪ] (*adv.*) 特殊地
succeed [səkˋsid] (*v.*) 成功
acceptable [əkˋsɛptəbḷ] (*adj.*) 可接受的
unique [juˋnik] (*adj.*) 獨特的
individual [ˌɪndəˋvɪdʒuəl] (*n.*) 個人
talented [ˋtæləntɪd] (*v.*) 有才能的
conservative [kənˋsɜvətɪv] (*adj.*) 保守的
miss out 錯失……

My own answer

Q72

How long do you expect to remain employed with our company?

你預期會在本公司待多久？

A1 有力簡答
 Track 73

I am a loyal employee and would like to remain employed here as long as I can still make a positive contribution to the company.

我是個高忠誠度的員工，只要我還可以帶給公司正面的貢獻，我都會想留在貴公司工作。

A2 深入詳答

Well, as you can see on my CV, I stayed in previous companies for quite a long time. I consider myself a pretty loyal employee. The more I understand your company, the more confident I am that my abilities and experience would be a good match to the position. So I would like to remain employed here as long as I can still make a positive contribution to the company.

嗯，如您在我的個人簡歷上可以看到的，我在之前公司都待得蠻久的。我自認為是個高忠誠度的員工。對貴公司了解越多，我就越有把握我的能力和經驗可以與這個職位相稱。因此，只要我還可以帶給公司正面的貢獻，我都會想繼續在貴公司工作。

Tips 面試一點通！

這是一個頗難回答的問題，卻也是外商雇主很有可能直接提出的問題。面試官想藉此了解應徵者的反應能力如何。這道問題沒有標準答案，只需照實回答說未來的事很難預測即可，但別忘了告訴對方，只要有可以貢獻己力的一天，一定會全力以赴。

Useful Expression 必通實用句型

I would like to remain employed here as long as I can make a positive contribution to the company.

只要我還可以帶給公司正面的貢獻，我都會想留在貴公司工作。

Power Vocabulary 好用字彙

loyal [ˋlɔɪəl] (adj.) 忠誠的
contribution [ˌkɑntrəˋbjuʃən] (n.) 貢獻

positive [ˋpɑzətɪv] (adj.) 正面的；積極的
employee [ˌɛmplɔɪˋi] (n.) 員工；雇員

✎ My own answer

Q 73 >

Tell me why you are the best candidate for this job. Can you give us a reason to hire you?

請說明你為什麼是這份工作的最佳人選。能否給我們一個雇用你的理由？

A1 有力簡答 （以銷售業務職缺為例）

 Track 74

I believe I am the best candidate because I have sales experience, excellent communication skills, and outstanding English language ability.

我相信我是最佳人選，因為我有業務經驗、良好的溝通技巧，和優秀的英文語言能力。

A2 深入詳答

You should hire me for three major reasons. The first reason is I have excellent sales skills. I have three years of sales experience and have achieved outstanding sales records. My clients like to buy things from me because I always maintain good relationships with them. The second reason you should hire me is related to my communication ability. I have received comprehensive and solid training in presentation and negotiation skills. Finally, you should hire me because of my bilingual ability. I am able to speak both Chinese and English fluently so I have confidence to help you expand the international market.

基於三個主要理由您應該雇用我。第一是因為我的銷售能力很強。我有三年的銷售經驗，並曾締造優秀的業績紀錄。我的客戶都很喜歡跟我做生意，因為我一直都和他們保持良好的關係。第二個您應該雇用我的原因和我的良好溝通能力有關。我接受過完整、扎實的簡報和談判技巧訓練。最後，因為我有雙語能力所以您應該雇用我。我會講流利的中、英語，我有信心可以協助貴公司拓展海外市場。

Tips 面試一點通！

回答此題可將自己的優勢或長處再強調一次，當然必須是跟工作相關、可以為公司創造利潤，而非只是一般的個人特質。

Useful Expression 必通實用句型

I believe I am the best candidate because I have [adjective / noun] experience, [adjective / noun] skill, and [adjective / noun] ability.

我相信我是最佳人選，因為我有〔形容詞／名詞〕經驗、〔形容詞／名詞〕技能，和〔形容詞／名詞〕能力。

Power Vocabulary 好用字彙

candidate [ˋkændəˌdet] (n.) 候選人
major [ˋmedʒɚ] (adj.) 主要的
relate to 跟……有關
solid [ˋsɑlɪd] (adj.) 扎實的
bilingual [baɪˋlɪŋgwəl] (adj.) 雙語的
expand [ɪkˋspænd] (v.) 拓展

outstanding [ˋautˋstændɪŋ] (adj.) 傑出的
relationship [rɪˋleʃənˌʃɪp] (n.) 關係
comprehensive [ˌkɑmprɪˋhɛnsɪv] (adj.) 廣泛的
negotiation [nɪˌgoʃɪˋeʃən] (n.) 談判
fluently [ˋfluəntlɪ] (adv.) 流利地

✎ My own answer

Q74

Are you active in community affairs? If so, please describe your participation.

你積極參與社區活動嗎？如果是的話，請描述你如何參與。

I participate in community affairs from time to time. For example, I volunteered in the city library, reading story books to children.

我不時會參與社區活動。比方，我曾在圖書館當志工，唸故事書給小朋友聽。

A2 深入詳答

Yes, I participate in community affairs from time to time as I want to establish trusting mutual relationships with others and I think these networks are valuable. In the past, I was involved with helping children in the community with their studies, and I think it really means something to me personally. And now, I spend my weekend volunteering and helping children to read in the city library. When I read stories to children, I get a sense of pride and think it's the best way to give back to the community.

是的，我不時會參與社區活動，因為我希望能夠與別人建立互信的關係，而我認為這些人際網路很有價值。過去，我曾幫助社區的兒童學習，我認為這對我個人而言很有意義。現在我則利用週末的時間當志工，在市立圖書館協助兒童閱讀。當我唸故事給孩子們聽的時候，我感到很自豪，我想這是回饋社區最好的方法。

Tips 面試一點通！

企業除獲利之外，也都很注重企業形象，有機會便會回饋社會。老闆藉由此問題可了解，應徵者在每日例行上下班之外，是否還有投入公共服務工作的熱忱。若是可以提出一兩個參與的公共活動，對應徵者會有加分效果。

Useful Expression 必通實用句型

In the past, I was involved with [doing something], and I think it really means something to me personally.

過去，我曾參與〔某事〕的經驗，我認為這對我個人來說真的很有意義。

Power Vocabulary 好用字彙

participate [pɑr`tɪsə,pet] (v.) 參與
form time to time 不時；有時
trusting [`trʌstɪŋ] (adj.) 信任的
network [`nɛt,wɜk] (n.) 網狀系統
involve [ɪn`vɑlv] (v.) 牽涉；使專注
give back to 回饋……

community affair 社區活動
establish [ə`stæblɪʃ] (v.) 建立
mutual [`mjutʃʊəl] (adj.) 雙方的
valuable [`væljʊəbl] (adj.) 珍貴的
sense of pride 自豪感

✏ My own answer

Q75

Do you consider yourself a leader or a follower?

你認為自己是領導人才還是部屬人才？

A1 有力簡答

 Track 76

I am enthusiastic, always like to motivate other colleagues, and more of a goal-orientated person, so I would consider myself a person with leadership potential.

我很熱心，總是喜歡激勵其他同事，並且比較是以目標為導向的人，因此，我自認為是具備領導潛力的人。

A2 深入詳答

Well, I consider myself both a leader and a follower, and it really depends on situations. But based on my previous experience, I am more of a leader. At Best Technology, I was not only enthusiastic about my own work, but I also motivated other associates. And whenever I faced some situations of uncertainty, I could react in a more orderly manner. Also, I viewed a situation as a whole and kept my focus on achieving the main goal. So based on these qualities, I would say I am more of a leader.

嗯，要視狀況而定，我認為個人可以是領導人也可以是部屬。但是根據我之前的經驗，我比較偏向是領導人才。在 Best 科技時，我不僅對自身的工作有熱情，也會激勵其他同事。只要面臨到不確定的狀況，我能夠做出有條理的反應。另外，我做事會顧全大局，將焦點放在完成主要的目標上。根據這些特質，我會認為自己算是領導型的人才。

Tips 面試一點通！

在一個企業團體內，一定會有領導者，也會有做事、執行的人。因此，只須依照自己的性格、興趣及專長等條件，誠實地告知雇主自己是偏向喜歡帶領他人，還是喜歡聽命行事即可。

Useful Expression 必通實用句型

I was not only enthusiastic about my own work, but I also motivated other associates.

我不僅對自身的工作有熱情，也會激勵其他的同事。

Power Vocabulary 好用字彙

enthusiastic [ɪnˌθjuzɪˋæstɪk] (*adj.*) 熱心的
goal-oriented [ˋgolˋorɪɛntɪd] (*adj.*) 目標導向的
associate [əˋsoʃɪˌet] (*n.*) 同事
orderly [ˋɔrdəlɪ] (*adj.*) 有條理的
achieve [əˋtʃiv] (*v.*) 達成

motivate [ˋmoteˌvet] (*v.*) 激勵
depend on 依……狀況而定
uncertainty [ʌnˋsɜtntɪ] (*n.*) 不確定性
as a whole 整體上

✎ My own answer

Q76

What is the most important thing our company can do to help you achieve your objectives?

什麼是我們公司幫助你達成目標可以做的最重要的事？

A1 有力簡答 （以業務人員訓練需求為例）

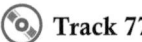 **Track 77**

I would need the company to provide me with necessary training in sales skills and good quality sales leads to follow up. And I would say that incentives could also be a good way to motivate sales reps.

我需要公司提供我必要的銷售技巧訓練及準確的潛在客戶名單讓我可作後續追蹤。另外，我也認為提供獎勵是個激勵業務人員的好辦法。

A2 深入詳答

As I am still fresh, I want to learn how to surpass my sales quota, close bigger deals, shorten the sales cycle, and make more money for both the company and myself. In order to achieve all these, I need the company to offer me training in sales skills and sales strategies. Also the company may need to plan some sort of demand generation activities in order to generate sales leads for me to follow up. Finally, I think the company can use incentives to motivate sales personnel to perform better.

因為我還是社會新鮮人，我想學習如何能超越我的業績額度，完成較大的交易，縮短銷售週期，並且讓公司與我個人都能賺到更多的錢。為了要達到這些目標，我需要公司能提供銷售技巧和業務策略的教育訓練。還有公司或許需要規劃能激發客戶需求的活動以創造潛在客戶讓我可以作後續追蹤。最後，我想公司可用獎勵方式來激勵業務人員有更好的表現。

Tips 面試一點通！

所謂「巧婦難爲無米之炊」，公司要請人來爲公司做事，當然不會讓員工單打獨鬥。若公司不提供相關資源，要員工拿什麼去打仗？因此，這道問題就是讓員工自己提出，除了自己的能力之外，還希望公司可以提供什麼樣的協助，以便更有效率地達到目標。答案可能是希望公司提供教育訓練、精準的客戶名單或激發需求的行銷活動等，應徵者可依自己的產業特性提出說明即可。

Useful Expression 必通實用句型

I need the company to offer me training in [something] and [something].

我須要公司提供給我〔某事〕和〔某事〕的訓練。

Power Vocabulary 好用字彙

sales lead 潛在客戶
incentive [ɪn`sɛntɪv] (n.) 獎勵
fresh [frɛʃ] (adj.) 新進的
sales quota 業績額度
sales cycle 銷售週期
perform [pə`fɔrm] (v.) 表現

follow up 把……貫徹到底；後續追蹤
motivate [`motə‚vet] (v.) 激勵
surpass [sə`pæs] (v.) 超越
shorten [`ʃɔrtən] (v.) 縮短
personnel [‚pɜsn̩`ɛl] (總稱) 員工

✏ My own answer

Q77

In what ways do you think the IT industry should change in order to be more competitive?

你認為資訊科技產業要做哪些個改變才能更有競爭優勢？

As more enterprise employees bring their own devices to work, I think the IT industry needs to pay more attention to mobile device management and security.

隨著有越來越多的企業員工都會帶自己的電子裝置去上班，我認為資訊科技業要更注意行動裝置的管理和安全性。

A2 深入詳答

Well, in order to make the IT industry more competitive, I think information security is the key. As a support engineer, I understand that enterprises consider that confidential business information is very critical, so they deploy security systems to protect information from modification, disclosure, or destruction. However, nowadays employees bring their own devices to work, such as smart phones, laptops, and tablets, so we IT people now face a new challenge to secure the company's confidential information. So I think as technologies keep improving, the IT industry needs to pay more attention to enterprise mobile device management.

嗯，為了讓資訊產業更有競爭力，我認為資訊安全是關鍵。身為一個資訊支援工程師，我了解企業主認為機密的商業資訊非常重要，所以他們會部署資訊安全系統來防止資訊遭篡改、洩露或破壞。然而，現在員工們帶自己的裝置，如智慧型手機、筆記型電腦和平板電腦等到公司，所以我們資訊人員現在面臨的新挑戰是要如何保護公司的機密資料。因此，我認為隨著科技不斷進步，資訊產業需要更關注企業行動裝置的管理。

Tips 面試一點通！

此題僅以資訊科技產業為例，若是應徵不同產業，則會有不同的問法，例如，若是保險業可能會問如何突破現狀，外銷產業可能會問如何找到更多客戶等。這類問題當然沒有標準答案，既然是要增加競爭優勢，回答的內容可以有多一點的創新和獨特見解。

Useful Expression 必通實用句型

I think as [something] keeps improving, a [adjective / noun] industry needs to pay more attention to [issue].

我認為隨著〔某事物〕一直在進步，〔形容詞／名詞〕產業需要更關注〔議題〕。

Power Vocabulary 好用字彙

enterprise [ˋɛntəˌpraɪz] (*n.*) 企業
mobile [ˋmobɪl] (*adj.*) 移動式的；行動的
confidential [ˌkɑnfəˋdɛnʃəl] (*adj.*) 機密的
protect [prəˋtɛkt] (*v.*) 保護；防護
disclosure [dɪsˋkloʒə] (*n.*) 洩露
laptop [ˋlæptɑp] (*n.*) 膝上型電腦
secure [sɪˋkjur] (*v.*) 使安全；保衛

device [dɪˋvaɪs] (*n.*) 設備；裝置
competitive [kəmˋpɛtətɪv] (*adj.*) 有競爭力的
critical [ˋkrɪtɪkl̩] (*adj.*) 緊要的；關鍵的
modification [ˌmɑdəfəˋkeʃən] (*n.*) 修改
destruction [dɪˋstrʌkʃən] (*n.*) 破壞
tablet [ˋtæblɪt] (*n.*) 平版電腦

✐ My own answer

Q78

If you could change something about your previous company, what would it be?

如果你可以改變之前公司的某些事，你會想改變什麼？

A1 有力簡答 （以客戶服務不周為例） **Track 79**

If I could, I would want to enhance their customer service schemes in order to increase their customer satisfaction rate.

如果可以的話，我會想提升他們的顧客服務機制，以提高他們的顧客滿意度。

A2 深入詳答

The previous company I worked for was an ERP software company and they provided high quality ERP solutions to enterprise customers. However, it seems to me that they neglected to provide good after-sale service and complete technical support. So if I could change something, I would want to improve their customer service systems and increase the customer satisfaction rate. All employees should pay more attention to and deal with customer complaints so that the company could benefit from good customer care.

我之前的公司是 ERP 軟體公司，他們提供高品質的 ERP 解決方案給企業客戶。但是在我看來，他們忽略了提供客戶良好的售後服務和完整的技術支援。因此，如果我可以做些改變，我會想改善他們的客戶服務系統，並提高客戶滿意度。公司內全體員工都應該更加注意和處理客戶抱怨，讓公司可以從做好客戶服務中獲益。

Tips 面試一點通！

員工會離職，很多時候是因爲前任公司某方面的做法與自己的理念不合或有落差，這道問題正好可反映出應徵者的心聲。回答時應以正面的角度出發，提出前公司若能做那些方面的改善即可變得更好。切忌只是一味批評或抱怨，應將焦點放在「可以改變的事」，意即如何讓公司變得更好的議題上。

Useful Expression 必通實用句型

If I could change something, I would want to improve [something] and increase [something].

如果我可以做些改變，我會想改善〔某事物〕和 並提高〔某事物〕。

Power Vocabulary 好用字彙

enhance [ɪn`hæns] (v.) 提高；增加
neglect [nɪg`lɛkt] (v.) 忽略；忽視
satisfaction [ˌsætɪs`fækʃən] (n.) 滿意
complaint [kəm`plent] (n.) 抱怨

scheme [skim] (n.) 計畫；方案
complete [kəm`plit] (adj.) 完整的
pay attention to 注意……
benefit [`bɛnəfɪt] (v.) 獲得好處

✏ My own answer

Q 79 >

How do you see this position being different from your past jobs?

你覺得這個職務和你前一份工作有什麼不同點？

A1 有力簡答　（以團隊工作為例）

 Track 80

Employees at my previous company worked alone, while your company emphasizes the importance of collaboration. For me, it's the major difference.

我之前公司的員工都是獨立作業，而貴公司則強調合作的重要性。對我來說這是主要的不同點。

A2 深入詳答

My previous employer, Wuta Company, was a relatively small company, so each employee worked individually and just focused on his or her own tasks. I know your company emphasizes the importance of team work, so I would say it's the major difference. For me, I will need to develop better collaborative skills as I will be working with other team members. For example, I need to listen attentively to other people's ideas, interact with the team, and communicate effectively in order to achieve shared goals. I believe I have the personality to become a successful team player.

我前任公司，五大企業，相對來說規模較小，因此每個員工都是獨立作業，只要專注做自己的工作就好。我了解貴公司強調團隊合作的重要性，我認為這就是主要的不同點。對我而言，我必須培養更好的合作能力，因為我將和其他團隊成員一起工作。比方說，我必須專注傾聽他人的意見、跟團隊互動，並做有效的溝通以完成共同目標。我相信我具備這樣的特質，可以成為成功的團隊成員。

Tips 面試一點通！

人是慣性的動物，一旦習慣做某件事後就會遵循之前的模式做下去。但是每家公司的情況不盡相同，不可能直接套用之前的工作模式照作就好。筆者在外商工作期間曾聽老闆提過，他最怕聽到員工做了錯誤決定後，丟出「以前我在某某公司這樣做也沒什麼問題呀！」這種反應，這樣只有更加凸顯自己不知變通的弱點。因此，遇到這個問題，應徵者可思考這份職務和前份工作的不同點，而自己應如何調適、融入新公司。

Useful Expression 必通實用句型

I know your company emphasizes the importance of [something], so I would say it's the major difference.

我了解貴公司注重的是〔某事物〕的重要性，所以我認為這就是主要的不同點。

Power Vocabulary 好用字彙

emphasize [ˋɛmfəˌsaɪz] (v.) 強調；著重
relatively [ˋrɛlətɪvlɪ] (adv.) 相較地；相對地
major [ˋmedʒɚ] (adj.) 主要的
interact [ˌɪntɚˋrækt] (v.) 互動
achieve [əˋtʃiv] (v.) 達成

collaboration [kəˌlæbəˋreʃən] (n.) 合作
individually [ˌɪndəˋvɪdʒʊəlɪ] (adv.) 單獨地
attentively [əˋtɛntɪvlɪ] (adv.) 聚精會神地
effectively [ɪˋfɛktɪvlɪ] (adv.) 有效地
personality [ˌpɝsṇˋælətɪ] (n.) 人格；個性

My own answer

Q 80 ▶

What skills or qualities do you think are important in this position?

你認為要做好這份工作哪些技能或特質很重要？

A1 有力簡答 （以廣告人員為例）　　　　　　 **Track 81**

I think a good advertising agent should possess marketing skills, be creative and persuasive, and be familiar with a variety of publicity media.

我認為一位好的廣告人員應該擁有行銷技巧、創意和說服力，並且要了解各種宣傳媒體。

A2 深入詳答

In order to be a good advertising agent, I think a person must possess marketing skills, be creative and persuasive, and be familiar with different types of publicity media. One of the main responsibilities of an advertising agent is to sell advertising, so he or she must understand the current market situation and relevant trends. And the person must be able to conceptualize an ad idea and satisfy clients' needs. Finally, the agent needs to distinguish the differences between various media, such as Internet ads, television ads, and newspaper ads. And I believe I can perform the job well, since I am innovative, familiar with different advertising media, and have sufficient marketing experience.

要成為一位出色的廣告人員，我認為要擁有行銷技巧、創意和說服力，並且要了解各種宣傳媒體。廣告人員的要務之一就是賣廣告，因此他或她須了解目前的市場狀況和相關趨勢。另外，也須要能夠將廣告的概念具體化並符合客戶的需求。最後，廣告人員必須了解各種宣傳媒體間的不同，比如網路廣告、電視廣告和報紙廣告等。我相信我可以勝任這份工作，因為我有創意、熟悉各種廣告媒體，也有豐富的行銷經驗。

Tips 面試一點通！

此問題非常明顯，老闆要應徵者思考一下，以公司的角度來看，需要何種技能才可勝任此此份工作。只要針對自己應徵的產業特性，提出應具備的技能即可。記得，不要只談論「我個人會什麼技能」，而要站在這家公司的角度來檢視及回答。

Useful Expression 必通實用句型

I believe I can perform the job well, since I am [adjective], familiar with different [something], and have sufficient [adjective / noun] experience.

我相信我可以勝任這份工作，因為我〔形容詞〕、熟悉各種〔某事物〕，也有足夠的〔形容詞／名詞〕經驗。

Power Vocabulary 好用字彙

advertising [ˋædvɚˌtaɪzɪŋ] (*n.*) 廣告業
possess [pəˋzɛs] (*v.*) 擁有；具備
persuasive [pɚˋswesɪv] (*adj.*) 具說服力的
media [ˋmidɪə] (*n.*) 媒體；工具
conceptualize [kənˋsɛptʃʊəlˌaɪz] (*v.*) 使概念化
distinguish [dɪˋstɪŋgwɪʃ] (*v.*) 分別；分辨
innovative [ˋɪnoˌvetɪv] (*adj.*) 創新的

agent [ˋedʒənt] (*n.*) 代理人；仲介
creative [krɪˋetɪv] (*adj.*) 有創意的
publicity [pʌbˋlɪsətɪ] (*n.*) 宣傳；宣傳品
current [ˋkɝənt] (*adj.*) 當前的
satisfy [ˋsætɪsˌfaɪ] (*v.*) 滿足
perform [pɚˋfɔrm] (*v.*) 表現
sufficient [səˋfɪʃənt] (*adj.*) 足夠的

✎ My own answer

Q81

Tell me about the salary range you are seeking.

請告知你希望待遇的範圍。

 Track 82

A1 有力簡答

Based on my experience and ability, I would say the range of a minimum of NT$40K to a maximum of NT$45K per month is reasonable.

就我的經驗和能力而言，我認為每個月薪資在最低四萬元台幣和最高四萬五千元台幣之間是合理的。

A2 深入詳答

Well, based on my experience and ability, I would say the range of a minimum of NT$40K to a maximum of NT$45K per month is reasonable. Also I need to know more details of the job description before I can propose an exact figure. But I'd like to emphasize that the paycheck is not the only factor for me to decide on a job. I believe it's more important to find the right position and the job I really have passion for.

嗯，就我的經驗和能力而言，我認為每月薪資在最低四萬元台幣和最高四萬五千元台幣之間是合理的。另外，我也需要知道此職位更多的細部內容，才能提出一個確切的數字。但我要強調，薪資並不是我選擇工作時唯一的因素。 我相信找到合適的職務和我對這份工作的熱忱才更為重要。

Tips 面試一點通！

此題可說是老闆必問的問題，但對應徵者來說又是難以拿捏的一道題目。談到薪資，若說得過低，怕自己的價值會被貶低；說得太多，又擔心給人獅子大開口的感覺。最好的解決方式就是在面談前要大約問一下周遭親朋好友在相關產業的合理薪資範圍。不一定是要一個明確的數字，可以是一個範圍，如此比較好跟未來的雇主討論。

Useful Expression 必通實用句型

Based on my experience and ability, I would say the range of a minimum of [amount] to a maximum of [amount] per month is reasonable.

就我的經驗和能力而言，我認為每月薪資落在最低〔金額〕和最高〔金額〕之間是合理的。

Power Vocabulary 好用字彙

salary range 薪資範圍

minimum [`mɪnəməm] (*adj./n.*) 最小限度（的）

reasonable [`riznəbl] (*adj.*) 有理的；合理的

propose [prə`poz] (*v.*) 提出；提議

emphasize [`ɛmfə͵saɪz] (*v.*) 強調；著重

factor [`fæktə] (*n.*) 因素

seek [sik] (*v.*) 尋求

maximum [`mæksəməm] (*adj./n.*) 最大限度（的）

job description 職務說明

figure [`fɪgjə] (*n.*) 數字

paycheck [`pe͵tʃɛk] (*n.*) 薪津；付薪水的支票

passion [`pæʃən] (*n.*) 熱情

My own answer

Q 82

If you knew your boss was 100% wrong about something, how would you handle it?

假若你知道你老闆對某事的判斷完全錯誤，你會如何處理？

A1 有力簡答

 Track 83

I would just raise the question in a private way, such as an email or a note, and let my boss consider proper solutions.

我會私下以像是電子郵件或紙條的方式提出問題，讓老闆思考適當的解決辦法。

A2 深入詳答

Well, I was lucky because my previous supervisor was an open-minded person and always welcomed new ideas. Whenever I told him "You know what? I think the project might go better if we changed our strategies to do this and that instead." He always replied, "Go ahead and just give it a try." But if my boss didn't like his authority questioned, I might just raise the questions and leave him to consider proper solutions. Once I get to know my boss well enough, I would want to collect sufficient information first and inform my boss of the potential downsides to his decision, in a more private way, of course.

嗯，我還滿幸運的，我的前任主管是個開明的人，非常樂於接受新的意見。每當我跟他說「你知道嗎？我認為這個案子改成這樣或那樣做的話，可能會進行地更順利。」他總是回答「那你就試試吧。」但是如果我的老闆不喜歡他的權威受到質疑，那我可能只會將問題提出，讓他自行思考適當的解決辦法。一旦我比較了解老闆的個性，我會先將資料收集齊全，然後告知老闆他的決定可能的不利之處，當然，會是透過私下的方式。

Tips 面試一點通！

這題會依每個人的性格差異而會有不同的答案。有話直說的人可能會直接了當地告訴老闆；含蓄內斂的人可能為求人際和諧不會當場明說，而會再找其他時機把意思傳達給老闆。這題一樣沒有標準答案，全視個人偏好哪一種處理方式，只要照實回答即可。

Useful Expression 必通實用句型

If my boss didn't like his authority questioned, I might just raise the questions and leave him to consider proper solutions.

如果我老闆不喜歡他的權威受到質疑，那我可能只會將問題提出，讓他自行思考適當的解決辦法。

Power Vocabulary 好用字彙

raise [rez] (v.) 提出
consider [kən`sɪdə] (v.) 考慮；細想
open-minded [`opən`maɪndɪd] (adj.) 開明的
potential [pə`tɛnʃəl] (adj.) 潛在的

private [`praɪvɪt] (adj.) 私下的
previous [`privɪəs] (adj.) 在前的；之前的
authority [ə`θɔrətɪ] (n.) 權威
downside [`daʊn͵saɪd] (n.) 不利

✎ My own answer

Q83

How do you propose to compensate for your lack of experience?

你打算如何補足經驗不足的部分？

A1 有力簡答

 Track 84

I would like to work closely with a mentor and ask a lot of job-related questions. I will also take necessary training courses after work. I am a quick learner and very willing to learn new things.

我很希望能跟一位前輩密切合作，並多詢問與工作相關的問題。我也願意利用下班時間進修必要的訓練課程。我學得很快並且非常願意學習新的事物。

A2 深入詳答

I understand that your company requires at least two years of experience in the advertising field. As I am still fresh, I am passionate about the job and very willing to learn everything. It would be wonderful if I could work closely with a mentor in the beginning and ask a lot of job-related questions. In addition, I am willing to take necessary training courses after work or on the weekends. I always welcome new challenges and can quickly absorb new concepts, so I am confident that I can start to bring your company great benefits within a short period of time.

我了解貴公司要求至少在廣告業有兩年的工作經驗。因為我是新進人員，我對這份工作充滿熱忱並且非常願意學習新的事物。我很希望一開始能跟一位前輩密切合作，並多詢問工作相關的問題。另外，我也願意利用下班或週末進修必要的訓練課程。我樂於接受挑戰也能很快吸收新知，因此我有信心可在短時間之內就能開始為公司做出貢獻。

Tips 面試一點通！

有不足無妨，重要的是該採取什麼行動來彌補不足。可先表明自己有開放的態度和上進心學習新的事物，之後再列出幾個自己可採取的行動，比方說上進修課程、向有經驗的人討教，或是多參考報章期刊上的案例等。換言之，應表達願意藉多方面的管道來增進自己的實力。

Useful Expression 必通實用句型

As I am still fresh, I am passionate about the job and excited to learn everything.

雖然我是新進人員，我對工作充滿熱情，我也對學新東西感到很興奮。

I will take necessary training courses after work. I am a quick learner and very willing to learn new things.

我願意利用下班時間進修必要的訓練課程。我學得很快並且非常願意學習新的事物。

Power Vocabulary 好用字彙

propose [prə`poz] (*v.*) 打算；計畫
mentor [`mɛntə] (*n.*) 良師益友
advertising [`ædvə,taɪzɪŋ] (*n.*) 廣告業
passionate [`pæʃənɪt] (*adj.*) 有熱情的

compensate [`kɑmpən,set] (*v.*) 補償
require [rɪ`kwaɪr] (*v.*) 要求；需要
fresh [frɛʃ] (*adj.*) 新來的；新進的
absorb [əb`sɔrb] (*v.*) 吸收

✎ My own answer

Q 84

Do you think you are overqualified for this position?

你會不會認為這份工作對你來說是大材小用？

A1 有力簡答  Track 85

I think I am fully qualified for this position. With my strong ability and experience I can start to achieve more for the company than someone with less experience.

我認為自己完全符合此份工作的資格。以我豐富的能力和經驗，我能夠比那些較沒經驗的人更快替公司做出貢獻。

A2 深入詳答

Well, I wouldn't say I am overqualified for this job. Instead, I think I am fully qualified. Before our interview, I researched a lot about your company and the position, and believe that I have the right skills required for this job. In addition, with my strong ability and experience I can start to achieve more for the company than someone with less experience. Most importantly, your company can benefit since you don't need to provide me with extra training. Anyway, the key point is that I do want to grow with your company, and salary and title are secondary to me.

嗯，我並不認為自己是大材小用，相反的，我認為自己完全符合此份工作的資格。在來此面談之前，我已對貴公司和這個職務做了很多功課，我相信我已具備這份工作所需的能力。另外，以我豐富的能力和經驗，我能夠比那些較沒經驗的人更快替公司做出貢獻。更重要的是，這對貴公司也有利，因為您不需再提供我額外的訓練。總之，重點是我想和貴公司一同成長，薪資和頭銜對我來說倒是次要的事。

Tips 面試一點通！

這是個非常直接了當的問題。回答時端視應徵者個人的心態，若眞的認爲是大材小用，薪資也和自己設想的有差距，也無須勉強。但若應徵者眞的對工作很有興趣，可以抱著虛心學習的心態，而且不在乎薪水多寡，那也要表明態度，畢竟你的最終目標就是得到這份工作。

Useful Expression 必通實用句型

With my strong ability and experience I can start to achieve more for the company than someone with less experience.

以我我豐富的能力和經驗，我可以比那些較沒經驗的人更快替公司做出貢獻。

Power Vocabulary 好用字彙

overqualified [ˋovəˋkwɑlə͵faɪd] (*adj.*) 條件過好的
achieve [əˋtʃiv] (*v.*) 達成
title [ˋtaɪtl] (*n.*) 頭銜
secondary [ˋsɛkən͵dɛrɪ] (*adj.*) 次要的

✍ My own answer

Q85

What are some of the things you find difficult? Why?

你做什麼樣的事情會覺得有困難？為什麼？

When under pressure, I have difficulty memorizing complicated information. I try to link the information to something that has occurred in my life, and it helps me to memorize things more easily.

在壓力之下，要記憶太過複雜的資訊對我會有些困難。我嘗試將資訊和我生活中發生的事連結，這樣我會比較容易將資訊記牢。

A2 深入詳答

Well, in the past I had difficulty memorizing a lot of complicated information. Especially when I was preparing for some sort of test, I found it even more difficult to memorize things under pressure. I've worked on some approaches to improving this and found that if I draw links from information to something that has occurred in my own life, it can be easier to memorize the information. Also I utilize my planner well and carry it with me at all times so I can make sure I don't miss out any important tasks.

嗯，過去要記住許多過於複雜的訊息我會有點困難。尤其是當我要準備某些考試時，我發現在壓力之下更難將資訊記憶下來。我試過一些增加記憶力的方式，我發現如果將資訊和我生活中發生的事連結，我會比較容易將該資訊記下來。另外，我也利用我個人的行事曆並隨身帶著它，以確保不會錯過任何重要的工作。

Tips 面試一點通！

人不是萬能的，因此針對此問題無需迴避，直接提出自己做起來有困難的事情。但也不需長篇大論講太多，點到即可，說得太多反而像是把自己的缺點放大來討論似的。重要的是必須強調自己會如何改善，以期今後可做得更好的辦法上。

Useful Expression 必通實用句型

I have difficulty [doing something].
我在〔做某事〕方面有困難。

Power Vocabulary 好用字彙

under pressure 在壓力之下
complicated [ˋkɑmpləˌketɪd] (adj.) 複雜的
occur [əˋkɝ] (v.) 發生
planner [ˋplænə] (n.) 個人行事曆
task [tæsk] (n.) 任務；工作

memorize [ˋmɛməˌraɪz] (v.) 記憶
approach [əˋprotʃ] (n.) 方法
utilize [ˋjutḷˌaɪz] (v.) 利用
carry [ˋkærɪ] (v.) 攜帶

✏ My own answer

Q 86

Do you know anyone who works at our company?

你認識我們公司任何員工嗎？

A1 有力簡答

 Track 87

Peter Hu in sales is my friend. He encouraged me to apply for this position, but still it is my own decision. The more I learn about this job, the more I like it.

業務部的 Peter Hu 是我的朋友。他鼓勵我來申請這個職缺，但最終還是我自己做出這個決定。越了解這份工作，我就越喜歡這份工作。

A2 深入詳答

Well, actually I know Peter Hu in your sales department. He highly recommended your company and that's why he encouraged me to apply. Still I would like to stress that I am making this decision on my own. After understanding more about your company, I really like it and believe I can use my skills in sales to benefit your company. Also I think Peter could be a good mentor and it would be wonderful if Peter could provide me with some valuable suggestions in the future.

嗯，事實上，我認識你們業務部的 Peter Hu。他極力推薦貴公司，也因此鼓勵我申請這個工作。但是我還是要強調，做決定的是我自己。再更了解貴公司之後，我真的很喜歡貴公司，也相信我的業務技巧可以為貴公司帶來貢獻。另外，我認為 Peter 今後可以當我的良師，如果他可以提供一些寶貴的建議給我，那就再好不過了。

Tips 面試一點通！

老闆會問此問題是因爲若應徵者有認識公司內部員工的話，就比較方便做 reference check（資歷查核）。另外，很多外商也有內部員工推薦人才的獎勵制度，若有認識的人的話也比較好照應，讓新人能更快進入狀況。當然，若沒有認識的人其實也無妨，憑藉著自己的實力取得工作的經驗將更可貴。

Useful Expression 必通實用句型

I know [someone] in your [department]. He encouraged me to apply for this job, but still I am making this decision on my own.

我認識你們〔部門〕的〔某人〕。他鼓勵我來申請這個工作，但是做決定的還我自己。

Power Vocabulary 好用字彙

apply [ə`plaɪ] (v.) 申請
encourage [ɪn`kɜɪdʒ] (v.) 鼓勵
benefit [`bɛnəfɪt] (v.) 帶來益處
suggestion [sə`dʒɛstʃən] (n.) 建議；提議

recommend [ˌrɛkə`mɛnd] (v.) 推薦
stress [strɛs] (v.) 強調
mentor [`mɛntə] (n.) 良師益友

✎ My own answer

Q 87

Are you applying for other jobs?
你是否同時還在找其他的工作？

 Track 88

In fact, yes, I am applying for a position in Company ITT, Company CCA, and the job here. I am interested in this position the most.

事實上，是的，我也有應徵 ITT 公司、CCA 公司的職位，以及貴公司的這個職缺。我對貴公司的職缺最感興趣。

A2 深入詳答

Well, to be honest with you, yes, I am applying for two other jobs. I am applying for positions at Company ITT, Company CCA, and the job here. Among all three, I am interested in this position the most. Not only do I have right qualifications, skills, and experience to fit the job, but I also like your company style and environment very much. I would like to make a decision within this month. If you need me to provide any other materials, like references or work samples, to help you decide, please feel free to let me know.

嗯，說實話，有的，我同時還應徵其他兩個工作。我申請 ITT 公司、CCA 公司的職缺，以及貴公司的職缺。在這三個當中，我對貴公司的工作最感興趣。除了我的資歷、技能和經驗跟這個工作相符，我也很喜歡貴公司的風格和環境。我想在本月內做出決定。如果您需要我提供其他任何資料，比如推薦人或作品集等，好幫助您做決定的話，請隨時通知我。

Tips 面試一點通！

此題可依應徵者自己的求職進度回答。另外，老闆也可以從答案中聽出應徵者所找的其他工作機會都是偏向哪個產業的，如此可對求職者多一分了解。

Useful Expression 必通實用句型

To be honest with you, yes, I am applying for positions at [company name], [company name], and the job here. Among all three, I am interested in this position the most.

說實話，有的，我申請〔公司名稱〕、〔公司名稱〕的職缺，以及貴公司的職缺。在這三個當中，我對貴公司的工作最感興趣。

Power Vocabulary 好用字彙

qualification [ˌkwɑləfəˋkeʃən] (n.) 資格；能力
style [staɪl] (n.) 風格
material [məˋtɪrɪəl] (n.) 文件資料；素材
reference [ˋrɛfərəns] (n.) 推薦；推薦人；推薦函
work sample 作品集

✏ **My own answer**

Q88

What will you do if you don't get this position?

若沒得到此工作，你的下一步為何？

 Track 89

I would ask the interviewer to give me some constructive feedback so that I can keep improving myself. Also I will take more training if necessary.

我會請面試官給我一些建設性的意見回饋，讓我可以不斷進步。另外，如果需要的話，我也願意多上些訓練課程。

A2 深入詳答

I probably will feel a bit disappointed. But I will take this interview as a valuable experience and keep sharpening my interview skills in order to perform well next time. Also I will ask the interviewer to tell me what my weak points are and give me some constructive feedback so that I can learn how to make my next interview more compelling. If I am not selected because I lack some necessary skills, I would like to seek more training before my next move.

我可能會覺得有點失望，但是我還是會把這次面談視為寶貴的經驗，並不斷精進面談技巧，以期下次可以有好的表現。另外，我也會請面試官告訴我我的弱點為何，並給我一些建設性的意見回饋，讓我在下次面談時表現得更有說服力。如果我是因為缺乏某些技能而沒被錄取的話，在我規劃下一步之前，我會先去上相關的訓練課程。

Tips 面試一點通！

此題是筆者在某大外商公司參與面談時聽到老闆提出的問題。想當然爾，知名美商軟體公司的工作競爭相當激烈，因此，老闆不免想知道在百中選一的情況下，應徵者若是不幸落選的那一位，接下來他或她會做什麼。一般人可能會回答「繼續再找其他工作」，但多數老闆想聽到的，其實應該會是像「若沒得到這份工作，我想請您不吝告訴我不足的部分是什麼，我好從這次機會中了解自己的盲點和弱點，以求日後好好補足改進。」這類的答案。因為能自我要求、不斷追求進步的人才，才是老闆心中的第一選擇。

Useful Expression 必通實用句型

I will ask interviewer to give me some constructive feedback so that I can keep improving myself.

我會請主考官給我一些建設性的意見，讓我可以不斷進步。

Power Vocabulary 好用字彙

constructive [kən`strʌktɪv] (adj.) 建設性的
disappointed [ˌdɪsə`pɔɪntɪd] (adj.) 失望的
perform [pɚ`fɔrm] (v.) 表現
compelling [kəm`pɛlɪŋ] (adj.) 令人信服的

feedback [`fid͵bæk] (n.) 意見回饋；反饋
sharpen [`ʃɑrpn̩] (v.) 精進；使敏銳
weak point 弱點
seek [sik] (v.) 尋求；追求

✎ My own answer

Q89

Is there anything else you would like to tell us?

你還有什麼想補充的嗎？

I would like to stress my achievements at CAI Corp. I received the GM Award for three consecutive years for my good performance. And I am sure I could make a positive contribution to your company as well.

我想要強調我在 CAI 公司的成就。因為表現優異，我連續三年榮獲「總經理獎」。我也非常確定我可以為貴公司帶來正面的貢獻。

A2 深入詳答

I would like to tell you more about my achievements at CAI Corp. I was responsible for channel marketing and developing strategies to increse product awareness and drive revenue. I led a team to arrange a series of events, campaigns, trainings, and promotion activities. Eventually our sales increased by 15% and customer satisfaction jumped by 27%. For all these achievements, I received the GM Award for three consecutive years. Since I was involved in the marketing strategy and dealt a lot with communications, this period working with CAI Corp. was the most important milestone in my life in terms of both professional and personal development.

我想進一步說明我在 CAI 公司的成就。我當時負責通路行銷並且必須為提升產品能見度和增加獲利制定策略。我帶領一個團隊規劃了一系列的活動、訓練及促銷方案。最後，我們的業績提升了百分之十五，而客戶滿意度也躍升了百分之二十七。正因為這些成就，我連續三年榮獲「總經理獎」。由於我參與了行銷策略並負責處理大量的溝通工作，在 CAI 公司工作的這段期間，可以說是我工作職涯專業和個人發展最重要的里程碑。

Tips 面試一點通！

這是老闆擔心之前的面談有所遺漏，而想讓應徵者再度強調自己優勢的最佳機會。既然有這種好機會，當然要好好地把握。不要只說「沒有要補充的」就結束面談；相反地，可以再次將自己的優勢、能為公司帶來的利益，和自己對此工作的興趣等再強調一次，讓老闆知道自己真的很有決心想要獲得這份工作。

Useful Expression 必通實用句型

I would like to tell you more about my [achievements] at [company name].

我想要進一步說明我在〔某公司〕的〔能力／成就〕。

Power Vocabulary 好用字彙

achievement [əˋtʃivmənt] (n.) 成就
make contribution to 為……做出貢獻
awareness [əˋwɛrnɪs] (n.) 察覺；體認
revenue [ˋrɛvəˌnju] (n.) 收益
customer satisfaction 顧客滿意度
in terms of 就……而論

consecutive [kənˋsɛkjʊtɪv] (adj.) 連續的
channel marketing 通路行銷
drive [draɪv] (v.) 驅動
campaign [kæmˋpen] (n.) 活動
milestone [ˋmaɪlˌston] (n.) 里程碑

✎ **My own answer**

Q 90

Do you have any questions for me?
你有沒有任何想問我的問題？

A1 有力簡答
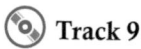 Track 91

I'd like to know if you offer opportunities for training. How do you evaluate employees' performance? And what's your company's management style?

我想知道您是否會提供教育訓練？貴公司如何評核員工表現？還有貴公司的管理風格為何？

A2 深入詳答

Well, I would like to thank you for your time first. And I want to emphasize that I am interested in this job and think I am well qualified for it. In the mean time, I do have a few questions. I'd like to know if you offer opportunities for training. And how do you evaluate employees' performance? Also could you describe your company's management style, please?

嗯，首先我要謝謝您的時間。我還是想強調我對此工作很有興趣，也認為自己可以勝任愉快。當下我的確還有些問題想請教。我想知道貴公司是否會提供教育訓練？貴公司如何評核員工表現？還有，是否可請您說明一下貴公司的管理風格？

Tips 面試一點通！

此題目是大部分老闆在面談最後都會問應徵者的一道問題。老闆主要是想藉此了解應徵者在提問方面的能力。另一方面，也可藉此了解求職者心中在意的是哪些事物，是一些無關緊要的細節，還是會以宏觀的角度來看待問題？切記提問務必要與工作相關，比方說教育訓練、出差機會、客戶類型或產品區隔等。（請參考〈Part 6 應徵者適合提出的問題與結束感謝用語〉）

Useful Expression 必通實用句型

I do have a few questions. I'd like to know if you [do something]?
我的確有幾個問題。我想知道貴公司是否〔做某事〕？

Power Vocabulary 好用字彙

evaluate [ɪˋvæljuˌet] (v.) 評估；評核
management style 管理風格
be interested in 對……有興趣
describe [dɪˋskraɪb] (v.) 描述

performance [pɚˋfɔrməns] (n.) 表現
emphasize [ˋɛmfəˌsaɪz] (v.) 強調
qualified [ˋkwɑləˌfaɪd] (adj.) 符合資格的

✎ My own answer

 **精選好用句型，一次入袋！**

　　學完本單元的高頻問題及擬答後，試著寫下自己的答案，最後再複習一次本單元的好用句型，有助於在面試時靈活套用，秀出最好的一面！

▶ **強調對應徵公司有做過功課**

☐ **In reviewing your company website, I've familiarized myself with your company mission and objectives.**
在審視過貴公司的網站後，我對貴公司的使命和目標有了更深的認識。

▶ **說明幾年後的工作期許**

☐ **I hope that I will have developed the competencies and experience to be considered for a [position].**
我希望我已具備可以勝任〔職位〕的能力和經驗。

▶ **說明何時可開始上班**

☐ **Please allow about [number of days] to transfer my responsibilities to colleagues at my current employer.**
請給我大約〔天數〕的時間，讓我可以把目前在公司負責的工作交接給其他同事。

▶ **說明短期目標**

☐ **My short-term objectives are to [do something] and [do something] within [time period.]**
我短期內的目標是在〔期限〕以內〔做某事〕並〔做某事〕。

▶ **說明達成短期目標方式**

☐ **Besides the [training courses] I am taking, I would also like to obtain real hands-on experience by [doing something].**
除了我目前在上的〔課程名稱〕外，我也想藉由〔做某事〕得到實務經驗。

▶ **說明應徵此份工作的原因**

☐ **I am good at [doing something], and I want to apply my skills to benefit your company.**
我擅長〔做某事〕，我希望能運用我的技能來幫助公司。

☐ **I would like to remain employed here as long I can make a positive contribution to the company.**
只要我還可以帶給公司正面的貢獻，我都會想留在貴公司工作。

▶ 說明為何自己是最佳人選

☐ **I believe I am the best candidate because I have [adjective / noun] experience, [adjective / noun] skill, and [adjective / noun] ability.**
我相信我是最佳人選，因為我有〔形容詞／名詞〕經驗、〔形容詞／名詞〕技能，和〔形容詞／名詞〕能力。

▶ 說明可勝任應徵工作的原因

☐ **I believe I can perform the job well, since I am [adjective], familiar with different [something], and have sufficient [something] experience.**
我相信我可以勝任此份工作，因為我〔形容詞〕、熟悉各種〔某事物〕，也有足夠的〔某事物〕經驗。

▶ 說明希望待遇

☐ **Based on my experience and ability, I would say the range of a minimum of [amount] to a maximum of [amount] per month is reasonable.**
就我的經驗和能力而言，我認為每月薪資落在最低〔金額〕和最高〔金額〕之間是合理的。

▶ 新鮮人或經驗不足者適用句型

☐ **As I am still fresh, I am passionate about the job and excited to learn everything.**
雖然我是新進人員，我對工作充滿熱情，我也對學新東西感到很興奮。

▶ 被質疑自己大材小用時適用

☐ **With my strong ability and experience I can start to achieve more for the company than someone with less experience.**
以我豐富的能力和經驗，我可以比那些較沒經驗的人更快替公司做出貢獻。

NOTES

Part 5

情境假設與機智問題

Hypothetical Situations and Problem Solving

Q 91

If you had enough money to retire right now, would you?

假使你現在有足夠的錢可以退休，你是否會現在就退休？

A1 有力簡答 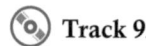 Track 92

No, I would not retire now even if I had enough money. I want to keep working because I am eager to look for more opportunities for my career growth and at the same time contribute my knowledge to society.

不會，即便現在我有足夠的錢我也不會想退休。我想繼續工作，因為我想找尋更多職涯成長的機會，同時也可以將自己所學回饋社會。

A2 深入詳答

Well, let me see. Although money plays an important role in my life and motivates me to work, I still think money is not everything. So, I would not retire now even if I had enough money. I still would like to keep working since I am eager to look for more opportunities for personal accomplishment, career growth, and social relationships. I would like to develop more different skills and enrich my own life, as well as be able to contribute my knowledge to help others in the community.

嗯，讓我想想。雖然錢對生活來說扮演著重要的角色，也是驅使我工作的動力，但是我還是覺得錢不會是全部。因此，即使我已有足夠的錢，我也不會退休。我仍然會繼續工作，因為我很想找尋更多增進個人成就、職涯成長和社會關係的機會。我想發展更多不同的技能來豐富自己的生命，同時貢獻一己之力來幫助社會上其他的人。

Tips 面試一點通！

關於「情境假設」或「機智問答」這類題目並不一定會與工作直接相關，面試官會提出這類題目，通常是想了解應徵者對一般性議題的看法。而由應徵者的答案不僅可測試應徵者的臨場反應能力，甚至可以了解他或她對生活的態度，以及分析事物或資訊連結的能力。上述這道題目便可了解應徵者對工作的態度爲何，是只爲了生活才工作，還是有其他目的。因此，答案不要只繞著錢打轉，而應說明工作本身對你的意義，或是可以帶來哪些超越金錢的價值。

Useful Expression 必通實用句型

I want to keep working because I am eager to look for more opportunities for [something] and at the same time contribute my knowledge to society.

我想繼續工作，因為我想找尋更多〔某事物〕的機會，同時也可以將自己所學回饋社會。

Power Vocabulary 好用字彙

retire [rɪ`taɪr] (*v.*) 退休
motivate [`motə͵vet] (*v.*) 激勵
enrich [ɪn`rɪtʃ] (*v.*) 使豐富

eager [`igə] (*adj.*) 渴望的；急切的
accomplishment [ə`kɑmplɪʃmənt] (*n.*) 成就
community [kə`mjunətɪ] (*n.*) 社區；社會

✎ My own answer

Q92

If you were hiring a person for this job, what would you be looking for?

如果要你雇用一個人來做這份工作,你會找哪種特質的人?

A1 有力簡答 (以業務代表為例)
 Track 93

I would be looking for someone with good communication skills, ambition, and willingness to keep learning.

我會找有良好溝通技巧、具有抱負和願意持續學習的人。

A2 深入詳答

If I were hiring a person for this sales representative position, I would be looking for someone who has excellent communication skills, who can communicate with a variety of clients. Also, I would want someone who has outstanding presentation and negotiation skills in order to present our products and solutions to customers and close deals. And of course, as a sales representative, ambition is equally important and the person should be willing to learn from others within the organization.

若是要我為這個業務代表職缺找人,我會找有優異溝通技巧、能跟各式各樣的客戶溝通的人。另外,我也會想找有傑出簡報和談判技巧的人,這樣可以將公司產品或解決方案介紹給客戶並完成交易。當然,作為業務代表,企圖心很重要,而且這個人應該要願意向組織內的同事討教學習。

Tips 面試一點通！

此問題很明顯地是面試官希望應徵者能以老闆的角度，設身處地站在公司思考，此份職缺需要具備哪些特質或能力。

Useful Expression 必通實用句型

I would be looking for someone with [something], [something], and [something].

我會找有〔某事物〕、〔某事物〕和〔某事物〕的人。

Power Vocabulary 好用字彙

ambition [æmˋbɪʃən] (*n.*) 抱負；野心
communicate [kəˋmjunəˌket] (*v.*) 溝通
outstanding [ˋautˋstændɪŋ] (*adj.*) 傑出的；優秀的
equally [ˋikwəlɪ] (*adv.*) 相等地

sales representative 業務代表
a variety of 各式各樣的
negotiation [nɪˌgoʃɪˋeʃən] (*n.*) 談判
willing [ˋwɪlɪŋ] (*adj.*) 願意的；樂意的

✎ My own answer

Q 93

What is your definition of success?
你對成功的定義為何？

I think my individual success depends on if I can achieve important personal goals.

我認為我個人的成功與否，端視自己是否能達成自己所設的重要目標而定。

A2 深入詳答

I do think that individual success mainly depends on whether a person can achieve important personal goals. I mean success is like a competition with ourselves rather than with something external, such as status and wealth. For example, my mother is a homemaker. It's not a high-status job, and she didn't earn a lot of money, but she feels satisfied, and thinks she is successful. She always says that her goals are to take good care of the family, so I think it is her dedication to the family that gives her a sense of success.

我深信個人成功與否端視其是否達成自己所設的重要目標而定。我意思是說，成功就是自己跟自己的比賽，而不是跟一些諸如地位、財富等外在條件相較來論定。比方說，我母親是一位家庭主婦，這個工作並沒有很高的社會地位，她也沒賺很多錢，但是她感到很滿足，也認為自己很成功。她總是說她的目標就是要照顧好整個家。因此，我認為就是這種為家庭奉獻的心讓她有成就感。

Tips 面試一點通！

成功爲何並沒有標準答案，端看個人對成功的定義。有人認爲生活快樂就是成功，而有人認爲功成名就才算成功。回答時可視自身情況，或思考自己向來注重生活的哪一部分或層面，來構思回答。

Useful Expression 必通實用句型

For me success is like a competition with myself rather than with something external.

對我來說，成功是自己跟自己的競賽，而不是跟外在條件相較來論定。

Power Vocabulary 好用字彙

individual [ˌɪndəˈvɪdʒuəl] (*adj.*) 個人的
competition [ˌkɑmpəˈtɪʃən] (*n.*) 競爭
status [ˈstetəs] (*n.*) 地位
homemaker [ˈhomˌmekə] (*n.*) 家庭主婦
dedication [ˌdɛdəˈkeʃən] (*n.*) 奉獻

achieve [əˈtʃiv] (*v.*) 達成
external [ɪkˈstɜnəl] (*adj./ n.*) 外在的／外在
wealth [wɛlθ] (*n.*) 財富
take care of 照顧……

✎ My own answer

Q 94 ▶

Do you prefer to live in a small town or a big city?

你喜歡住在小鎮上還是大都市？

 **Track 95**

I like to live in a big city, because it has developed transportation systems, plenty of activities to do, and more medical facilities.

我喜歡住在大都市，因為都市有較完善的大眾交通系統、很多的活動，還有較多的醫療設施。

A2 深入詳答

I personally prefer to live in a big city. I am currently living in Taipei, and I can find plenty of malls around my neighborhood, where I can buy everyday necessities. Also I think in big cities, medical facilities and emergency services are more easily accessible than in the countryside. Big cities also have convenient transportation systems. In addition, there are always plenty of social activities, sports events and concerts. In the countryside, however, life may be too quiet and dull, and I may only have a few neighbors. Living alone with few activities might cause some mental problems.

我個人比較喜歡住在大都市。我目前住在台北市，住家附近就有很多購物中心，可以買到每日的生活必需品。另外，我認為大都市的醫療設施和緊急服務比在鄉下地方更容易取得。大都市還有便利的交通系統，除此之外，還有許多的社交活動、體育賽事和音樂會等。但是在鄉下，生活可能會太安靜且無趣，而且鄰居可能也不多。獨自生活又沒有什麼活動可參與，可能會引起一些精神方面的問題。

Tips 面試一點通！

有些公司位於大都會區之中，有些公司則位於小鎮上。老闆藉由此問題可了解應徵者偏好哪種生活型態，也藉此來判斷應徵者是否可以融入未來的工作環境。

Useful Expression 必通實用句型

In big cities, [something] are more easily accessible than in the countryside.

在大都市內，〔某事物〕比在鄉下地方更容易取得。

Power Vocabulary 好用字彙

transportation [ˌtrænspəˈteʃən] (*n.*) 交通
facility [fəˈsɪlətɪ] (*n.*) 設備；設施
mall [mɔl] (*n.*) 購物中心
necessity [nəˈsɛsətɪ] (*n.*) 必需品
countryside [ˈkʌntrɪˌsaɪd] (*n.*) 鄉間
dull [dʌl] (*adj.*) 無趣的

medical [ˈmɛdɪkl] (*adj.*) 醫療的
currently [ˈkɜəntlɪ] (*adv.*) 目前
neighborhood [ˈnebəˌhʊd] (*n.*) 社區
accessible [ækˈsɛsəbl] (*adj.*) 可取得的
concert [ˈkɑnsət] (*n.*) 演奏會；音樂會

✎ My own answer

Q 95

Do you always tell the truth?
你總是說實話嗎？

A1 有力簡答

 Track 96

I always tell the truth in the workplace. But if the situation requires, I might tell a white lie for the benefit of other people.

我在工作場所向來都是實話實說。但若情況需要，我可能會為了他人的利益著想而說個無惡意的小謊。

A2 深入詳答

Well, to be honest, it really depends on different situations. I understand that people generally think that telling the truth is no doubt the most important consideration in any situation. Indeed, "Honesty is the best policy." And the foundation of any relationship is truth. In business environment I always tell the truth. However, always telling the truth may not be a good idea, especially in a situation where it is better not to reveal the truth for the benefit of other people. So, I might sometimes tell a white lie in order to make other people feel better.

嗯，老實來說，這真得視不同情況而定。我了解一般來說大家都認為，說實話毫無疑問是在任何情況之下最重要的事。的確，「誠實是最好的策略。」，而且誠實也是所有關係最重要的基石。在商務環境中，我只說實話。但是老是實話實說也未必都是個好主意，尤其是在為了他人的利益著想最好不要說出實話的時候。因此，我有時候可能會說個無惡意的小謊來讓他人覺得好過些。

Tips 面試一點通！

這是一個很微妙的問題，並不容易回答。若說自己從未說過謊，似乎不太可能，但若答自己常不說實話，又欠妥當。因此，最好的策略就是不要正面回答 "yes" 或 "no"，而說要視狀況而定。若能舉不同場合的實例來說明自己的因應之道會更好。

Useful Expression 必通實用句型

I might do [something] for the benefit of other people.
為了他人著想，我會〔做某事〕。

Power Vocabulary 好用字彙

workplace [`wɜk,ples] (n.) 工作場所
benefit [`bɛnəfɪt] (n.) 利益；好處
consideration [kənsɪdə`reʃən] (n.) 需要考量的事
foundation [faun`deʃən] (n.) 基礎

white lie 無惡意的小謊言；白色謊言
generally [`dʒɛnərəlɪ] (adv.) 一般來說
policy [`pɑləsɪ] (n.) 策略；原則
reveal [rɪ`vil] (v.) 揭露；揭開

My own answer

Q 96 ▸

How do you deal with office politics and gossip?

你會如何面對辦公室政治和八卦？

A1 有力簡答 **Track 97**

To deal with office politics, I always stay calm and consider how to react. As for office gossip, I just concentrate on my own job and stay out of it.

針對辦公室政治，我總是保持鎮定並會思考該如何應對。至於辦公室八卦，我就只專注在自己的工作上，置身事外。

A2 深入詳答

To deal with office politics, I always try to stay cool, calm, and collected, and take time to consider how to react. And I tend to be flexible and positive. One real example is that while I was working at ABC Company three years ago, a junior coworker got a promotion over me. Instead of acting right on my emotions, I took some time to think and decided to voice my opinion. I consulted with my boss about what actions I can take in order to improve my performance. I didn't make it personal; I just focused on action items that I could control. As for gossip, well, I just focus on reality and try not to participate in office gossip.

面對辦公室政治，我總是保持平靜、淡定，並會花點時間思考如何應對。我傾向保持彈性和正面思考。舉個實例，三年前當我在 ABC 公司工作時，有個較資淺的同事獲得升遷的職位高於我。當時我並沒有馬上做出情緒反應，我花了一些時間思考，並決定說出自己的心聲。我向老闆諮詢，我能做什麼來改進我的表現。我並沒有把這件事視為是針對我個人，只專注在我可以控制的行動上。至於八卦，嗯，我只看事實，也盡可能不參與八卦討論。

Tips 面試一點通！

若說辦公室就是一個小型的社會，相信沒有人會反對。團體內有是非八卦是免不了的，就算不是發生在自己身上，身處同個辦公環境該如何看待辦公室政治或八卦，也是一門學問。老闆想藉由此問題了解應徵者在處理這方面問的解決能力。回答時除了描述自己的因應之道外，亦可舉出實例。

Useful Expression 必通實用句型

To deal with [something], I always try to stay [attitude] and take time to consider how to react.

面對〔某事〕，我總是試著保持〔某態度〕，並會花點時間思考如何應對。

Power Vocabulary 好用字彙

office politics 辦公室政治
react [rɪˋækt] (v.) 反應
concentrate [ˋkɑnsɛnˌtret] (v.) 專注；集中
flexible [ˋflɛksəbl] (adj.) 彈行的
promotion [prəˋmoʃən] (n.) 升遷
consult [kənˋsʌlt] (v.) 商議

calm [kɑm] (n.) 鎮靜的
office gossip 辦公室八卦
collected [kəˋlɛktɪd] (adj.) 鎮定的
positive [ˋpɑzətɪv] (adj.) 正面的
voice [vɔɪs] (v.) 說出；發聲
participate [parˋtɪsəˌpet] (v.) 參與

✎ My own answer

Q97

Do you tend to speak to people before they speak to you?

你是否會在別人跟你交談之前先跟人攀談？

  Track 98

Yes, I am an outgoing person so I tend to speak to people first. And I am a good listener too as I am interested in knowing more about what others are thinking.

是的，我是一個外向的人，所以我都會先跟別人說話。而我也是個好聽眾，因為我很有興趣多知道一些其他人的想法。

A2 深入詳答

I see myself as a good mixer, so yeah, I always speak to people first especially in the workplace. As a sales representative, whenever I have opportunities to meet with potential customers, I always concentrate on what to say, how to say it, and how to communicate my ideas better. In addition, I certainly understand that communication is not a one-way process. So even when I make the first move to speak to people, I am an active listener as well. I am also interested in what other people are thinking.

我自認是一個善於交際的人，所以，是的，我總是會先主動跟人談話，尤其是在工作場所。身為業務代表，只要我有機會跟潛在客戶見面，我總會專注於說話的內容、如何表達，以及如何更有效地傳達我的想法。此外，我當然了解溝通不是單向的過程而已。因此即便我先主動跟人交談，我也會積極傾聽他人的心聲。我也對其他人的想法很有興趣。

Tips 面試一點通！

面試官想藉此了解應徵者的個性是內向話少，還是外向活潑，並進一步推斷此人是否能勝任這項職務。比方說，要是不太喜歡主動和人談話的人，可能不太適合從事業務開發的工作。

Useful Expression 必通實用句型

Whenever I have opportunities to [do something], I always concentrate on [something].

只要我有機會做〔某事〕，我總是專注於〔某事〕。

Power Vocabulary 好用字彙

tend to 傾向於
potential [pə`tɛnʃəl] (*adj.*) 潛在的
one-way 單向的

good mixer 善交際的人
concentrate [`kɑnsɛn,tret] (*v.*) 專注；集中
active [`æktɪv] (*adj.*) 主動的；積極的

✎ My own answer

Q 98

If a client calls you with a question and you don't have the answer, what do you do?

如果有客戶打電話給你提了一個你無法回答的問題，你會怎麼辦？

A1 有力簡答

 Track 99

Insteading of saying "I don't know", I would find out the answer for the customer and get back to the customer as soon as possible.

我不會說出「我不知道」這種答案，我會盡力幫客戶找到解決辦法，並在最短的時間內回覆客戶。

A2 深入詳答

Well, in that situation, first of all I will tell the client the truth saying that I don't have an answer to his question at the moment. And then I will provide the client with some follow-up actions I can take, like, I will find out the answer, and get back to him within one hour. I think the key point here is that instead of saying "I don't know," I will definitely try my best to offer assistance to solve the client's problem.

嗯，在這種情況下，我會先跟客戶說實話，告訴對方我目前沒有他所要的答案。接下來我讓客戶知道隨後我會採取的行動為何，比方說，我會幫他找到解決方案，並在一小時內回覆他。我認為重點在於，我不會說「我不知道」，我一定會盡全力協助客戶解決他們的問題。

Tips 面試一點通！

為了做好客戶服務，即便第一時間沒有客戶想要的答案，也要盡力協助客戶
找到答案並解決問題。回答時態度也應明確，比方，不要說「我會盡快幫您
找答案」，而應該說「我會在十分鐘左右回覆您」，盡可能提出具體的說明，
展現出你想解決問題的誠意。

Useful Expression 必通實用句型

Instead of saying [something], I definitely will try my best to [do something].

我不會說〔某事〕，我一定會盡全力去〔做某事〕。

Power Vocabulary 好用字彙

find out 查明
follow-up [ˋfaloˌʌp] (adj.) 後續的
assistance [əˋsɪstəns] (n.) 協助

get back to 再與……說話（尤指電話上）
definitely [ˋdɛfənɪtlɪ] (adv.) 明確地；肯定地
solve [salv] (v.) 解決

✏ My own answer

Q 99

What is your philosophy towards work?
你的工作理念為何？

A1 有力簡答

 Track 100

My work philosophy is "Learn from mistakes and never give up."

我的工作理念是「從錯誤中學習，而且永不放棄」。

A2 深入詳答

My work philosophy is "Learn from mistakes and never give up." Once I entered the job market two years ago, it didn't take long for me to figure out that getting ahead wasn't simply about being good at what I could do. I realized that many hurdles would crop up in the workplace or even in my life. I see them as useful stepping stones to a better outlook in the workplace. So the key point is that whenever I make mistakes or encounter difficulities, instead of just giving up, I underline the reasons first and make a resolution to learn from them. I believe that I can accelerate self-improvement by learning from my own mistakes.

我的工作理念是「從錯誤中學習，而且永不放棄」。兩年前我進入職場後不久，我就了解到要有所進步不光是做好我會做的事。我體會到在職場甚至在生活上，一定會出現很多阻礙。我將這些阻礙視為對未來前景有助益的踏腳石。所以，重點是當我犯錯或面臨困難時，我不會放棄，相反的，我先將問題點找出來，然後謹記教訓。我相信從自己的錯誤學習，能加快自我進步的速度。

Tips 面試一點通！

老闆會想了解應徵者的理念和公司的理念是否契合；若是彼此理念差不多，往後自然合作愉快。在面談前，可以先在網路上對公司做一番徹底研究，看看應徵公司的理念或企業文化為何，面試時就會比較容易發揮。

Useful Expression 必通實用句型

I believe that I can accelerate self-improvement by learning from my own mistakes.

我相信從自己的錯誤學習，能加快自我進步的速度。

Power Vocabulary 好用字彙

philosophy [fə`lɑsəfɪ] (n.) 理念；哲理
figure out 想出；算出
realize [`rɪə͵laɪz] (v.) 了解；體會
crop up 突然出現
outlook [`aʊ͵lʊk] (n.) 前景
underline [͵ʌndɚ`laɪn] (v.) 標出；強調
accelerate [æk`sɛlə͵ret] (v.) 加速

job market 職場
get ahead 獲得成功
hurdle [`hɝdl] (n.) 障礙；跳欄
stepping stone 踏腳石
encounter [ɪn`kaʊntɚ] (v.) 遇到
resolution [͵rɛzə`luʃən] (n.) 決心；果斷力

✎ My own answer

Q100

When an issue is raised during a meeting, do you tend to jump right in and offer your opinion or sit back and think it through before you talk?

在會議中某個議題被提出時，你傾向馬上加入討論並提供自己的看法，還是會先仔細思考然後再發言？

A1 有力簡答  Track 101

Well, in this situation, I think it through before making any comments in order to avoid potential misunderstandings.

嗯，在這種情況下，我會先想清楚再發言，以避免可能產生的誤解。

A2 深入詳答

When an issue is raised during a meeting, I tend to think it through before I offer my opinion. I don't want to just blurt out the first thing that comes into my mind without thinking twice. Instead, I like to think through the issue, have some possible solutions in mind and also think carefully about the words I use. This way I will be able to avoid any potential misunderstandings. I think if I just go ahead and voice my half-baked thought, colleagues won't value my opinions that much.

當會議中某個議題被提出時，我傾向先仔細思考再提出自己的看法。我不想未經思考就脫口說出當下閃過腦中的意見。相反地，我會將問題仔細想過一遍，在腦中想出一些可能的解決方案，我也會斟酌我的用詞。這樣我就可避免掉一些無謂的誤解。我認為如果我直接說出思慮欠周的想法，同事並不太會看重我的意見。

Tips 面試一點通！

由此狀況題可以看出應徵者是急於表達意見的人，還是深思熟慮的人。雖說每個人的性格或作風不同，但在職場上，想說就說的行事風格很可能會在無意間得罪人或踩到他人地雷，因此還是以顧及他人感受的說話方式較爲妥當。

Useful Expression 必通實用句型

I think it through before making any comments in order to avoid potential misunderstandings.

我會先想清楚再發言，以避免可能產生的誤解。

Power Vocabulary 好用字彙

think through 仔細想過

misunderstanding [ˌmɪsʌndə`stændɪŋ] (n.) 誤解

offer one's opinion 提供某人的意見

possible [`pɑsəbḷ] (adj.) 可能的

half-baked [`hæf bekt] (adj.) 【口】思慮欠周的；不完整的

avoid [ə`vɔɪd] (v.) 避免

raise [rez] (v.) 提出（問題、意見等）

blurt out 脫口說出

voice [vɔɪs] (v.) 說出；表達

✎ My own answer

 **精選好用句型，一次入袋！**

　　學完本單元的高頻問題及擬答後，試著寫下自己的答案，最後再複習一次本單元的好用句型，有助於在面試時靈活套用，秀出最好的一面！

▶ 說明「若自己是老闆，會雇用何種特質的人」

☐ **I would be looking for someone with [something], [something], and [something].**
我會找有〔某事物〕、〔某事物〕和〔某事物〕的人。

▶ 說明「對成功的定義」

☐ **I think my individual success depends on if I can achieve important personal goals.**
我認為個人的成功與否端視自己是否能達成自己所設的重要目標而定。

▶ 說明「如何面對辦公室政治或八卦」

☐ **To deal with office politics, I always stay calm and consider how to react. As for office gossip, I just concentrate on my own job and stay out of it.**
面對辦公室政治，我總是保持鎮定並會思考該如何應對。至於辦公室八卦，我就只專注在自己的工作上，置身事外。

▶ 說明「客戶提出沒有解答的難題，會如何解決」

☐ **Insteading of saying "I don't know," I would find out the answer for the customer and get back to the customer as soon as possible.**
我不會說出「我不知道」這樣的答案，我會盡力幫客戶找到解決辦法，並在最短的時間內回覆客戶。

▶ 說明工作理念

☐ **My work philosophy is "Learn from mistakes and never give up."**
我的工作理念是「從錯誤中學習，而且永不放棄」。

▶ 說明失敗經驗對你的意義

☐ **I believe that I can accelerate self-improvement by learning from my own mistakes.**
我相信從自己的錯誤學習，能加快自我進步的速度。

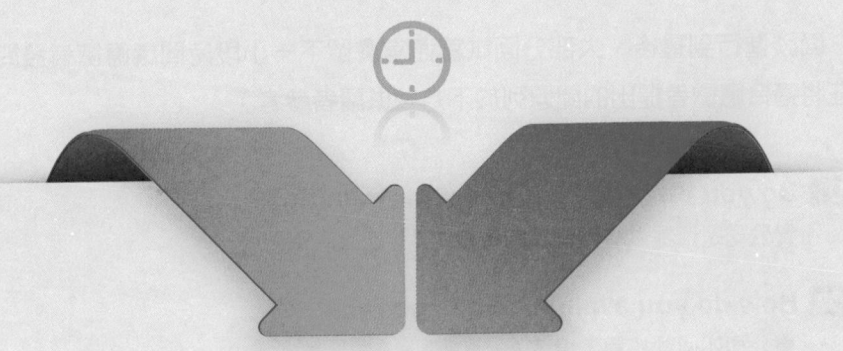

Part 6
應徵者適合提出的問題與結束感謝用語
The Applicant's Questions and Ending the Interview

應徵者適合提出的問題

 **Track 102**

面談進行到最後，大部分面試官通常會留下一小段時間讓應徵者發問，現在將適合應徵者提出的問題列於下方，供讀者參考：

Q1 Do you offer opportunities for training?
貴公司是否提供教育訓練的機會？

Q2 How do you evaluate employees?
貴公司如何評核員工績效？

Q3 How much travel is involved in this position?
這個職位出差的頻率為何？

Q4 May I know when you plan to make a hiring decision?
我可不可以知道貴公司何時會做出錄取決定？

Q5 Is the position based in Singapore, Hong Kong, or Taipei?
這個職缺是在新加坡、香港，還是台北？

Q6 Are salary adjustments geared to the cost of living or job performance?
薪資調整是依據生活水平還是個人表現？

Q7 Does your company encourage further education?
貴公司鼓勵在職進修嗎？

Q8 Is this a new position or am I replacing someone?
此工作是新職缺還是有人離職？

Q9 Do you fill positions from the outside or promote from within first?
貴公司如有職缺的話，是從外面找人還是先由內部人員提拔？

Q10 Could you describe your company's management style?
可以請您描述一下貴公司的管理風格嗎？

evaluate [ɪ`vɛljʊˌet] (v.) 對……評價；評核

hiring [`haɪrɪŋ] (n.) 雇用

adjustment [ə`dʒʌstmənt] (n.) 調整

further education 進修

fill [fɪl] (v.) 填補

management style 管理風格

travel [`trævl] (n.) 旅行；出差

base [bes] (v.) 以為基地

gear [gɪr] (v.) 使適應；使適合

replace [rɪ`ples] (v.) 取代

promote [prə`mot] (v.) 晉升

 結束感謝用語　　　　　　　　　　 Track 103

　　面談結束之後，面試官通常不會轉身就走，而是會利用一小段時間禮貌性感謝應徵者赴約，此時你也可以再次表達對老闆撥空與你面談的感謝之意。除了 "Thank you very much." 這句感謝詞之外，也可以使用下列句子：

❑ **Thank you for your time and I really enjoyed meeting you.**
謝謝您撥空，我真的很高興能跟您會面。

❑ **I really appreciate your consideration.**
我非常感激您考慮我的申請。

❑ **I really enjoyed our discussion.**
我非常高興與您的討論。

❑ **I really appreciate you giving me this time and opportunity to demonstrate my abilities.**
我很感激您撥空與我面談並給我這個機會證明我的能力。

❑ **Thank you for taking the time to describe the details of this position.**
謝謝您撥空跟我說明這個職位的細節。

另外，也可以表達想後續保持聯絡的心意。

❏ **If you need me to provide more information to help you decide, please feel free to let me know.**
若您還需要我提供任何資料來協助您做決定，請隨時通知我。

❏ **Let's keep in touch. Good-bye.**
讓我們就保持聯繫了，再見。

Section 3

面試好用詞彙補給

1 描述個人特質

優點字彙

1 **ambitious** [æmˋbɪʃəs] 形 有抱負的;有野心的
2 **dependable** [dɪˋpɛndəbl] 形 可靠的;可信任的
3 **energetic** [ɛnəˋdʒɛtɪk] 形 有活力的;精力旺盛的
4 **loyal** [ˋlɔɪəl] 形 忠誠的;忠心的
5 **realistic** [rɪəˋlɪstɪk] 形 注重現實的;現實的
6 **reliable** [rɪˋlaɪəbl] 形 可信賴的;可靠的
7 **respected** [rɪˋspɛktɪd] 形 受人尊敬的;受敬重的
8 **self-reliant** [ˋsɛlfrɪˋlaɪənt] 形 自立的;自恃的
9 **sincere** [sɪnˋsɪr] 形 真誠的;衷心的
10 **sophisticated** [səˋfɪstɪˌketɪd] 形 世故的;老練的
11 **articulate** [ɑrˋtɪkjəlɪt] 形 能言善道的;口才好的
12 **pioneering** [paɪəˋnɪərɪŋ] 形 先導的;開創的
13 **original** [əˋrɪdʒənl] 形 有獨創性的;新穎的
14 **aggressive** [əˋgrɛsɪv] 形 有企圖心的;有野心的
15 **lively** [ˋlaɪvlɪ] 形 活潑的;生氣勃勃的
16 **bold** [bold] 形 勇敢的;無畏的
17 **decisive** [dɪˋsaɪsɪv] 形 堅決的;果斷的
18 **mature** [məˋtjur] 形 成熟的;穩重的
19 **courteous** [ˋkɜtjəs] 形 謙恭的;有禮的
20 **productive** [prəˋdʌktɪv] 形 生產力高的;有成效的

弱點字彙

1 **inflexible** [ɪnˋflɛksəbl] 形 剛硬的;執拗的;不屈不撓的
2 **unforgiving** [ˌʌnfəˋgɪvɪŋ] 形 不原諒人的;無情的
3 **moody** [ˋmudɪ] 形 心情不穩的;喜怒無常的
4 **vain** [ven] 形 自負的;炫耀的
5 **gloomy** [ˋglumɪ] 形 憂鬱寡歡的;陰沉的
6 **trivial** [ˋtrɪvɪəl] 形 淺薄的;平凡的
7 **childish** [ˋtʃaɪldɪʃ] 形 孩子般的;幼稚的

8 **indifferent** [ɪnˋdɪfərənt] 彤 冷淡的；不關心的

9 **biased** [ˋbaɪəst] 彤 偏見的；存有成見的

10 **bossy** [ˋbɑsɪ] 彤 愛指揮他人的；跋扈的

11 **curt** [kɜt] 彤 唐突的；草率的

12 **restless** [ˋrɛstlɪs] 彤 焦躁不安的；靜不下來的

13 **impolite** [ˌɪmpəˋlaɪt] 彤 沒禮貌的；粗魯的

14 **lifeless** [ˋlaɪflɪs] 彤 枯燥無味的；了無生氣的

15 **naive** [nɑˋiv] 彤 天真的；輕信的

☛ 思考方式

1 **analytical** [ˌænlˋɪtɪkl] 彤 分析性的 (= analytic)

2 **creative** [krɪˋetɪv] 彤 有創意的；有創造力的

3 **imaginative** [ɪˋmædʒəˌnetɪv] 彤 富想像力的；有創意的

4 **logical** [ˋlɑdʒɪkl] 彤 有邏輯的；合理的

5 **objective** [əbˋdʒɛktɪv] 彤 客觀的；沒偏見的

6 **systematic** [ˌsɪstəˋmætɪk] 彤 有系統的；有條理的

7 **strategic thinking** 策略性思考

8 **critical thinking** 批判性思考

9 **innovative** [ˋɪnoˌvetɪv] 彤 創新性的；有開創性的

10 **constructive** [kənˋstrʌktɪv] 彤 有建設性的；有助益的

11 **penetrating** [ˋpɛnəˌtretɪŋ] 彤 尖銳的；有洞察力的

12 **diplomatic** [ˌdɪpləˋmætɪk] 彤 圓滑的；圓融的

13 **perceptive** [pəˋsɛptɪv] 彤 理解的；敏銳的

14 **discerning** [dɪˋzɜnɪŋ] 彤 有識別力的；聰敏的

15 **reasonable** [ˋriznəbl] 彤 合理的；通情達理的

☛ 工作能力

1 **adaptable** [əˋdæptəbl] 彤 適應力強的；能適應新環境的

2 **flexible** [ˋflɛksəbl] 彤 有彈性的；靈活的

3 **efficient** [ɪˋfɪʃənt] 彤 有效率的；有能力的

4 **methodical** [məˋθɑdɪkəl] 彤 有條理的；井然有序的

5 **resourceful** [rɪˋsorsfəl] 形 資源豐富的；足智多謀的

6 **tactful** [ˋtæktfəl] 形 機智的；圓滑的

7 **professional** [prəˋfɛʃən]] 形 專業的；很內行的

8 **mobile** [ˋmobɪl] 形 機動的；能快速移動的

9 **resilient** [rɪˋzɪlɪənt] 形 有彈力的；迅速恢復精力的

10 **experienced** [ɪkˋspɪrɪənst] 形 有經驗的；熟練的

11 **responsible** [rɪˋspɑnsəb]] 形 負責任的；有責任心的

12 **organized** [ˋɔrgən͵aɪzd] 形 有系統的；有組織力的

13 **self-motivated** [ˋsɛlf motɪvetɪd] 形 自動自發的；自發的

14 **hard-working** [͵hɑrdˋwɜkɪŋ] 形 努力工作的；勤勉的

15 **goal-oriented** [ˋgolˋɔrɪɛntɪd] 形 目標導向的

☛ 工作態度

1 **active** [ˋæktɪv] 形 積極的；主動的

2 **aggressive** [əˋgrɛsɪv] 形 進取的；有企圖心的

3 **alert** [əˋlɝt] 形 機警的；警覺的

4 **conscientious** [͵kɑnʃɪˋɛnʃəs] 形 憑良心的；盡責的

5 **disciplined** [ˋdɪsəplɪnd] 形 有紀律的

6 **enthusiastic** [ɪn͵θjuzɪˋæstɪk] 形 熱心的；熱忱的

7 **forceful** [ˋforsfəl] 形 強而有力的；堅強的

8 **practical** [ˋpræktɪk]] 形 講求實際的；實際的

9 **passionate** [ˋpæʃənɪt] 形 有熱情的；激昂的

10 **straightforward** [͵stretˋforwəd] 形 正直的；坦率的

11 **ingenuous** [ɪnˋdʒɛnjʊəs] 形 無邪的；率直的

12 **serious** [ˋsɪrɪəs] 形 嚴肅的；認真的

13 **persistent** [pɚˋsɪstənt] 形 堅持不懈的；持久的

14 **diligent** [ˋdɪlədʒənt] 形 勤奮的；勤勉的

15 **indefatigable** [͵ɪndɪˋfætɪgəb]] 形 不屈不撓的

2 說明興趣喜好

1 **gardening** [ˋgɑrdn͵ɪŋ] 名 園藝

2 **rock climbing** 攀岩

3 **reading** [`ridɪŋ] 名 閱讀

4 **watching movies** 看電影

5 **visiting friends** 拜訪朋友

6 **shopping** [`ʃɑpɪŋ] 名 逛街；購物

7 **yoga** [`jogə] 名 瑜珈 / **meditation** [ˌmɛdə`teʃən] 名 冥想

8 **jogging** [`dʒɑgɪŋ] 名 慢跑

9 **swimming** [`swɪmɪŋ] 名 游泳

10 **roller skating** 溜直排輪

11 **jumping rope** 跳繩

12 **surfing** [`sɜfɪŋ] 名 衝浪

13 **bicycling** [`baɪsɪk]ɪŋ] 名 騎單車

14 **cooking** [kʊkɪŋ] 名 烹飪

15 **dancing** [`dænsɪŋ] 名 跳舞

16 **diving** [`daɪvɪŋ] 名 潛水

17 **fishing** [`fɪʃɪŋ] 名 釣魚

18 **hiking** [haɪkɪŋ] 名 遠足；徒步旅行

19 **photographing** [`fotəˌgræfɪŋ] 名 攝影

20 **language learning** 學習語言

3 說明進修規劃

1 **advanced training** 進修訓練

2 **online course** 線上課程

3 **managerial position** 管理階層職位

4 **distance learning** 遠距教學

5 **real-world business application** 實際商場的應用

6 **information session** 說明會

7 **enhance leadership potential** 提升領導潛力

8 **intensive program** 密集課程

9 **EMBA** 企業管理碩士在職專班（為 Executive Master of Business Administration 簡稱）

10 **international accreditation** 國際認可（學校／課程等）

4 説明個人經驗 （動詞過去式）

👈 發想提議

1. **conceived** [kən`sivd] 構思；設想
2. **originated** [ə`rɪdʒə,netɪd] 創始引發
3. **planned** [plænd] 策劃
4. **programmed** [`progræmd] 編排；制訂
5. **proposed** [prə`pozd] 提議
6. **provided** [prə`vaɪdɪd] 提供
7. **introduced** [,ɪntrə`djust] 介紹
8. **devised** [dɪ`vaɪzd] 設計；策劃
9. **engineered** [,ɛndʒə`nɪrd] 策劃；建造
10. **invented** [ɪn`vɛntɪd] 發明
11. **designed** [dɪ`zaɪnd] 設計
12. **manufactured** [,mænjə`fæktʃəd] 製造
13. **automated** [`ɔtəmetɪd] 使自動化；使機械化
14. **specified** [`spɛsə,faɪd] 具體說明
15. **formulated** [`fɔrmjə,letɪd] 規劃；想出；配置

👈 創始開發

1. **created** [krɪ`etɪd] 創造
2. **generated** [`dʒɛnə,ret] 產生
3. **developed** [dɪ`vɛləpt] 開發；發展
4. **established** [əs`tæblɪʃt] 建立
5. **initiated** [ɪ`nɪʃɪ,et] 起始
6. **launched** [lɔntʃt] 啟動；開展
7. **pinpointed** [`pɪn,pɔɪntɪd] 定位；精確顯示
8. **perfected** [`pɜfɪktɪd] 使完美
9. **projected** [prə`dʒɛktɪd] 企劃；計劃
10. **improved** [ɪm`pruvd] 改善；增進
11. **visualized** [`vɪʒʊə,laɪzd] 設想；使形象化
12. **integrated** [`ɪntə,gretɪd] 整合

13 **progressed** [prə`rɛskt] 進行；進步

14 **executed** [`ɛksɪ,kjutɪd] 執行

15 **revolutionized** [,rɛvə`luʃən,aɪzd] 革新；改革

👉 領導管理

1 **administered** [əd`mɪnəstəd] 管理；執管

2 **approved** [ə`pruvd] 核可；認可

3 **conducted** [kən`dʌktɪd] 帶領；經營

4 **directed** [də`rɛktɪd] 指導；指揮

5 **guided** [`gaɪdɪd] 引導；指引

6 **led** [lɛd] 領導

7 **managed** [`mænɪdʒd] 管理；經營

8 **organized** [`ɔrgə,naɪzd] 組織；安排

9 **reorganized** [ri`ɔrgə,naɪzd] 重組；改組

10 **supervised** [`supəvaɪzd] 監督；管理

11 **structured** [`strʌktʃəd] 組織；建置

12 **empowered** [ɪm`pauəd] 授權；准許

13 **authorized** [`ɔθə,raɪzd] 授權；委託

14 **stimulated** [`stɪmjə,letɪd] 激勵；激發

15 **motivated** [`motɪvetɪd] 鼓勵；激發

👉 參與執行

1 **adopted** [ə`dɑptɪd] 採用；採納

2 **analyzed** [`ænḷ,aɪzd] 分析；解析

3 **conferred** [kən`fɜd] 授與；協商

4 **coordinated** [ko`ɔrdn̩etɪd] 協調；調和

5 **delegated** [`dɛləgɪtɪd] 委派

6 **evaluated** [ɪ`vælju,etɪd] 評估；評價

7 **implemented** [`ɪmpləməntɪd] 實施

8 **maintained** [men`tend] 維護；維持

9 **participated** [pɑr`tɪsə,petɪd] 參與；參加

10 **performed** [pə`fɔrmd] 執行；表現

11 **recommended** [ˌrɛkə`mɛndɪd] 推薦；建議

12 **reviewed** [rɪ`vjud] 複查；檢閱

13 **revised** [rɪ`vaɪzd] 校訂；修正

14 **supported** [sə`portɪd] 支持；支援

15 **scheduled** [`skɛdʒuld] 排程；安排時間

16 **set up** 設定；建立

17 **trained** [trend] 訓練；培養

18 **negotiated** [nɪ`goʃɪˌetɪd] 商討；協商

19 **articulated** [ɑr`tɪkjəletɪd] 明確有力地表達

20 **mandated** [mæn`detɪd] 命令；下指令

☞ 成效結果

1 **accelerated** [æk`sɛləˌretɪd] 加速；促進

2 **activated** [`æktəˌvetɪd] 活化；使活潑

3 **completed** [kəm`plitɪd] 完成；完結

4 **demonstrated** [`dɛmənˌstretɪd] 示範；證明

5 **effected** [ɪ`fɛktɪd] 造成；實現

6 **eliminated** [ɪ`lɪməˌnetɪd] 消除；淘汰

7 **expanded** [ɪk`spændɪd] 擴張；拓展

8 **expedited** [`ɛkspɪˌdaɪtɪd] 加速執行；促進

9 **improved** [ɪm`pruvd] 改進；改善

10 **increased** [ɪn`krist] 增加；增強

11 **influenced** [`ɪnfluənst] 影響；左右

12 **interpreted** [ɪn`tɝprɪtɪd] 說明；解釋

13 **reduced** [rɪ`djust] 縮減；降低

14 **reinforced** [ˌriɪn`fɔrst] 強化；增援

15 **revamped** [ri`væmpd] 更新；改造

16 **simplified** [`sɪmpləˌfaɪd] 簡化

17 **solved** [sɑlvd] 解決

18 **streamlined** [`strimˌlaɪnd] 流線化；簡化

19 **strengthened** [`strɛŋθənd] 加強；強化

20 **accomplished** [ə`kɑmplɪʃt] 達成；完成

附　錄

Supporting Documents
履歷表、求職信及後續追蹤信件範例

- 1. 履歷表 (Curriculum Vitae)
- 2. 求職信 (Cover Letter)
- 3. 後續追蹤信件 (Follow-up Letter)

☞ **範例 I**

已有「業務相關」經驗者要找「百貨經銷產業」管理職缺，範例如下：

Tiffany Liu

2020 Grand Avenue

Taipei, Taiwan 10411

(886) 2-2555-7000

Objective: Retail management position that allows for career growth.

WORK EXPERIENCE

6/2009 – Present　*Sales Manager, Good-Buys, Tainan, Taiwan*
Manage two dress departments and five coat departments.
Supervise and motivate thirteen associates.
Maintain excellent customer service.
Ensure proper merchandise presentation on sales floor.
Review and react to merchandise information reports, establishing trends and best-selling items.
Communicate with central merchants, store managers and sales personnel.
Control individual department inventory.
Management evaluation: "Excellent."

2/2007 – 6/2009　*Sales Coordinator, Sogo, Taipei, Taiwan*
Facilitated prompt flow of departmental merchandise.
Ensured accuracy of paperwork and inventory control.
Maintained efficient vendor and branch store communications.
Reviewed stock levels and merchandise assortment.
Tracked departmental trends.
Supervisor evaluation: "Superior performance."

7/2002 – 2/2007　*Secretary, Maximum's, Taipei, Taiwan*
Exposed to operational management.
Worked closely with assistant store managers.
Got familiar with compensation and insurance plans, payroll procedures, employee reviews, and customer service (including customer complaints and billing).
Performance evaluation: "Outstanding."

劉芬妮

10411 台灣台北市盛大路 2020 號

(886) 2-2555-7000

工作目標：具有職涯成長空間的零售管理職位。

經歷

6/2009 – 目前　　台灣，台南市／愛買百貨銷售經理

- 管理兩個時裝部門和五個大衣部門
- 監督並激勵十三位員工
- 維護良好客戶服務
- 確保銷售樓面上的商品展示恰當
- 審查並回應商品情報報告，建立趨勢與最暢銷商品品項
- 與主要零售商、店經理和銷售人員溝通
- 控管個別部門庫存
- 管理評核：「優等」

2/2007–6/2009　　台灣，台北市／ **SOGO** 太平洋百貨銷售協調專員

- 促進部門商品銷售流暢
- 確定書面作業的正確性與庫存控管
- 維持供貨商與分店溝通順暢
- 檢視庫存量與商品分類
- 追蹤百貨部門趨勢
- 督導評核：「表現卓越」

7/2002–2/2007　　台灣，台北市／麥克斯公司秘書

- 接觸營運管理
- 與商店副理合作密切
- 熟悉賠償與保險計畫、支薪程序、員工審核與客戶服務（包括客訴與開立帳單）
- 表現評核：「傑出」

剛自「商管」背景畢業者要找「電腦／管理產業」程式人員職缺，範例如下：

James Chen
29 Central Street
New Taipei, Taiwan, 80228
(886) 2-2895-5236

OBJECTIVE: Make a contribution using my proven abilities with computer programming.

EXPERIENCE HIGHLIGHTS:

HIGH-TECH COMPUTER PERIPHERALS, TAIPEI, 1999 – Present
DATA PROCESSING SUPERVISOR:
Responsible for overseeing the work of seven full-time and three part-time employees.
Coordinated, controlled, and directed the ordering, use, and maintenance of Unique-Tech Equipment.
Ensured accuracy and security of all data entry and output.
Accountable for the maintenance, operation, and performance of the Unique Data Communications Network for Taipei and all outside users in Taiwan.

TECHNICAL PROGRAMMER:
Responsible for the operation of Virtual Center.
Position required thorough knowledge of communication equipment.

EDUCATION:

University of Taipei – Taipei, Taiwan, B.A. Business Administration
Major: Management with emphasis on computer programming languages

AFFILIATIONS:

1997 – 1998 Student Group Director
1996 Student Chapter Chairperson
1995 Program Club Chairperson

PERSONAL ATTRIBUTES:

I am accustomed to accepting responsibility and delegating authority, and I am capable of working with people at all levels. I am able to plan, organize, develop, implement, and supervise complex programs and special projects.

陳力仁
80228 台灣新北市中央街 29 號
(886) 2-2895-5236

目標：發揮我在電腦程式方面的實力做出貢獻。

經歷摘要

高科技電腦周邊設備公司，台北市，1999 – 目前

資料處理部門主管：

- 負責管理 7 位全職與 3 位兼職員工
- 協調、控管並指導「獨一科技」儀器之訂購、使用及維護
- 確保所有資料輸入與輸出之正確與安全
- 負責台北與台灣境內所有區域用戶所屬「獨一資料通訊網路」之維護、運作與性能

技術性程式設計員：

- 負責虛擬中心的運作
- 該職位需要對通訊設備具完善之知識

教育程度

- 國立台北大學企業管理系學士／台灣，台北
- 主修：管理學（著重於電腦程式語言）

社團經驗

- 1997–1998 學生社團會長
- 1996 學生分會會長
- 1995 程式社團社長

個人特質

我熟習接受責任和分派職務，能與各階層的人共事。我有計畫、組織、開發、執行與監督複雜程式和專案的能力。

☛ **範例 III**

已有「軟體產業」工作經驗者尋求「產品經理」職位，範例如下：

Miller Wu

291 Fu-Hsing S. Road

Tao-Yuan, Taiwan, 38438

(886) 3-328-8462

Job Target: Product Manager

Experience

4/2007 ~ Present Scientific Software Inc., Tao-Yuan, Taiwan

☑ Senior Marketing Manager

☑ Duties include: Establish partnerships with software vendors (Citrix Systems, Salesforce.com, Oracle, etc.) and act as the main contact window for marketing plans and forecasts

1/2003 ~ 4/2006 SoftTech Taiwan Corporation, Taipei, Taiwan

☑ Assistant Partner Development Manager

☑ Duties included:

- In charge of channel marketing activities, including MSPP brand and value proposition.
- Gold / Certified partners conference, partner kick-off, and major events. VSAT 7.0+.
- Trial-Kit subscription reached 1,700 units. Top 3rd rev. in APAC, following AU and Japan.
- Partner incentive programs and activities: helped partners increase sales volume by 20%.

Education

8/07 ~ Present National Taiwan University, Taipei, Taiwan

📖 Master of Science / Major: Computer Science

On-Job Training

- Cisco / Microsoft / Citrix computer network systems related technical training courses.
- Information Systems related products sales / marketing tactics training courses.
- Advanced English, writing, reading, and critical reasoning training courses.
- Professional English speech / presentation skills training. (California Management Inst.)

Reference

Mr. Jacky Lee; GM of Scientific Software Inc.; 886-2-4736-7070; jacky-lee@scisoft.com

吳民樂

38438 台灣桃園市復興南路 291 號
(886) 3-328-8462

職務目標：產品經理

經歷

4/2007 ~ 目前　台灣，桃園市／科學軟體公司

☑ 資深行銷經理

☑ 職務包括：與軟體商（如：思傑系統、Salesforce.com、甲骨文等）建立合作關係，並在行銷企畫與市場預測上擔任主要聯繫窗口

1/2003 ~ 4/2006　台灣，台北市／台灣軟體科技公司

☑ 合作開發副理

☑ 職務包括：

- 負責行銷通路活動，包括：「微軟合作夥伴計畫」之品牌與價值提案

- 微軟黃金級認證夥伴會議，合作發起與主要會議，VSAT 7.0+.

- 試用套件認購達到 1,700 組，亞太地區收益排名第三，僅次於澳洲與日本

- 合作獎勵計畫與活動：幫助合作夥伴增加 20% 的銷售量

教育背景

8/07 ~ 目前　台灣，台北市／國立台灣大學

📖 理學碩士／主修：資訊工程

在職訓練

- 思科／微軟／思傑電腦網路系統相關之技術培訓課程
- 資訊系統相關產品之銷售與行銷策略培訓課程
- 高階英語寫作、閱讀與批判性推理培訓課程
- 專業英語演說／簡報技巧培訓（加州管理學院）

推薦者

科學軟體公司總經理李傑高先生 / Tel: 886-2-4736-7070 / email: jacky-lee@scisoft.com

777 Grand Ave.
Taipei, Taiwan, 10412

March 15, 2013

Mr. Jordan Yang
Human Resources Director
Data-Core Systems
111 2nd Blvd.
New Taipei, Taiwan 23483

Dear Mr. Yang,

I am writing to express my interest in applying for the Data Analyst position at Big-Data Systems. After reviewing your company website, I am quite excited about the possibility of working for your company. Your dedication to building a world-class team, providing top-notch analysis solutions, and offering excellent customer service is especially attractive to me. I believe that my abilities and interests match your company values, as demonstrated in my CV.

With my relevant professional experience in data mining, information management and market development, I believe I have the knowledge and skills to help empower Big-Data Systems to reach higher levels of productivity and efficiency. I am confident that my prior experience in analyzing huge amounts of market and customer data has provided me with the skills needed to become a successful data analyst at Big-Data Systems.

I enclose a copy of my CV for your review. I would greatly appreciate the opportunity to talk with you further about Big-Data Systems and the position. I will give you a call next week to see if there may be a convenient time to meet with you. Thank you for your time and consideration.

Sincerely,

Lisa Lo

10412 台灣台北市
廣太路 777 號

2013 年 3 月 15 日

楊喬登先生
人事部主任
資料核心系統公司
23483 台灣新北市第二大道 111 號

敬愛的楊先生，

我寫這封信的目的是想表達我有意應徵大大資訊系統公司資料分析師一職。在看過貴公司的網站後，我為在貴公司服務的可能性感到相當興奮。貴公司致力於建立一個世界級團隊、提供一流分析解決方案及優良客戶服務，這些對我都格外具有吸引力。我相信我的能力與興趣與貴公司的價值相符合，請參閱我履歷上的說明。

由於我在資料探勘、資訊管理與市場開發方面有相關的專業經驗，我相信我具備能幫助大大資訊系統公司達到更高層次之生產力與效率的知識和技能。我相信我先前在分析大量市場與客戶資料上的經驗讓我具備了必要的技能，足以在大大資訊系統公司擔任稱職的資料分析師。

附上我的履歷供您檢閱。如能有機會與您更進一步談談關於大大資訊系統公司與該職位，將不勝感激。下週我會致電給您，看看是否能找個方便的時間與您會面。感謝您的時間與考慮。

羅麗莎
敬上

777 Grand Ave.
Taipei, Taiwan, 10412

March 15, 2013

Ms. Julie Chen
Recruiting Manager
CIT Network Inc.
111 2nd Blvd.
New Taipei, Taiwan 23483

Dear Ms. Chen,

I am writing about the position of Technical Consultant that you advertised in *Technology Post*. As a technical support engineer with six years' experience, I believe I am well qualified for this position. You will see from the attached resume that I have experience in providing technical support to customers both on the phone and onsite. In many cases I have worked on, I was able to raise the standards of the troubleshooting procedure and increase customer satisfaction levels.

Having met and exceeded my goals in my previous position, I would like to challenge myself further with a more demanding position. The position of Technical Consultant in your company would give me this type of challenge.

After you've had a chance to look at my resume, please feel free to reach me at 0916-273-373 to schedule an interview. Thank you very much for considering my application.

Sincerely,

Mark Hsieh

10412 台灣台北市
廣太路 777 號

2013 年 3 月 15 日

陳珠麗女士
招募經理
CIT 網路公司
23483 台灣新北市第二大道 111 號

敬愛的陳女士，

我寫此封信是因為我想應徵貴公司在《科技報刊》上所刊登的技術顧問一職。我擁有六年技術支援工程師的經驗，我相信我完全能勝任這個工作。您從隨信附上的簡歷可看到，我有經透過電話或現場為客戶提供技術協助的經驗。在我處理過的許多案子中，我都能夠提高故障排除程序的標準，並提高客戶滿意度。

由於我在前個工作崗位上已達成且甚至超越了我的目標，我想進一步尋求要求更高的職務來挑戰自己。貴公司技術顧問的職位就能給予我此類型的挑戰。

在您有機會看過我的簡歷之後，請隨時與我聯繫以安排面試，我的電話是 0916-273-373。非常謝謝您考慮我的申請。

謝馬克
敬上

777 Grand Ave.
Taipei, Taiwan, 10412

March 15, 2013

Mr. Jordan Yang
Human Resources Director
Data-Core Systems
111 2nd Blvd.
New Taipei, Taiwan 23483

Dear Mr. Yang,

Recently I have been researching the leading companies in market analysis that are respected in the field. The name of Data-Core Systems keeps coming up as a top company.

As an experienced account manager, I have enough business background and a strong analytical approach to market changes. Furthermore, I am a competitive person professionally. Having exercised the talents and skills required to exceed goals and set records as a Sales Manager, I believe in measuring performance by results.

My resume is enclosed. I would appreciate the chance of a meeting to discuss my sales and management capabilities in detail. Please let me know if there is additional information I can provide that would lead you to schedule an interview.

Sincerely,

Lisa Lo

Enclosure

【譯文】

10412 台灣台北市
廣太路 777 號

2013 年 3 月 15 日

楊喬登先生
人事部主任
資料核心系統公司
23483 台灣新北市第二大道 111 號

敬愛的楊先生，

最近我一直在研究市場分析領域當中受到尊敬的幾個龍頭企業，「資料核心系統」這個名字不斷出現於頂尖公司之列。

身為一名經驗豐富的客戶經理，我具備足夠的商業背景，以及一套應付市場變化的牢固分析方法。此外，我在專業領域上非常具競爭力。在我擔任銷售經理時曾運用我的才華與技能，超越標地並締造佳績，我相信成果是衡量能力表現的準則。

隨信附上我的履歷。若能有機會碰面針對我在銷售和管理上的能力作細節的討論，本人將不勝感激 。如果有任何我可以提供的額外資訊以便您安排面談，請不吝通知。

羅麗莎
敬上

附件

☞ 範例 I

2020 2nd Blvd.
Taipei, Taiwan, 11037

September 18, 2013

Ms. Lily Chang
Human Resources Director
CCI Inc.
3829 Highland Ave.
Hsin-Chu, Taiwan 23483

Dear Ms. Chang,

I really enjoyed our discussion last week of the graphic designer position you want to fill.

I am grateful to know that my experience is definitely an asset. I trust you recognized my interest in the "graphic designer" position. My hope is that my competencies fit well with your requirements. I am eager to contribute my knowledge to the position, and believe that the extensive experience I've already had will make me a very suitable candidate.

Please find enclosed a list of references that you requested. I look forward to hearing from you regarding your hiring decision soon.

Thank you so much for your time and for the congenial interview.

Sincerely,

Wendy Chao

【譯文】

11037 台灣台北市
第二大道 2020 號

2013 年 9 月 18 日

張莉娟女士
人力資源中心總監
CCI 有限公司
23483 台灣新竹市高原路 3829 號

敬愛的張女士，

上禮拜我們針對貴公司增補平面設計師一職的會面讓我受益良多。

很感謝能夠知道我的資歷對貴公司會是一項有利的資產。相信您已了解我對「平面設計」這個
職位的關切，希望我的能力符合貴公司的要求。我渴望為這項職務貢獻我的才智，並且相信以
我所具備的豐富經歷，我應是非常合適的人選。

附件是您要求的推薦人名單。期待盡快收到您關於錄用決定的回覆。

非常感謝您的時間與那場融洽的面試。

趙溫蒂
敬上

3738 Hsing-Lung Rd.
Taipei, Taiwan, 10412

October 15, 2013

Mr. Steven Fu
Recruiting Manager

Best-Tech Inc.
111 Chi-Nan Street
Tainan, Taiwan 63483

Dear Mr. Fu,

Thank you for considering me for the Account Sales Manager position we discussed on October 13th. By way of verifying my continued interest in this opening, I'd like to emphasize the accomplishments I feel would ensure a level of performance fully in accord with your needs.

Recent accomplishments:
- ✔ As senior sales manager, I developed sales plans for the Taiwan region for the past five years.
- ✔ I developed sales strategies for enterprise virtualization deployment, netting more than $3.5 million in solution sales — a 20% market share.
- ✔ I had total sales responsibility for existing large enterprise accounts and prospective clients.

Again, thank you for your time, consideration and for all your efforts to arrange the interview. I am looking forward to hearing from you soon.

Sincerely,

Doris Yang

【譯文】

10412 台灣台北市
興隆路 3738 號

2013 年 10 月 15 日

傅義文先生
招募經理

貝司特科技公司
63483 台灣台南市齊南街 111 號

敬愛的傅先生，

關於我們於 10 月 13 日所討論之客戶銷售經理一職，感謝您能考慮由我來擔任。為了證實我在這個職缺上持續的關注，我想強調幾項水準表現我認為是與貴公司之需求充分相符的成就。

近期成就：
- ✔ 過去五年來我以資深業務經理的身分負責開發台灣地區的銷售計畫。
- ✔ 我為企業的虛擬化建置銷售策略，銷售解決方案淨賺超過三百五十萬美金，相當於百分之二十的市占值。
- ✔ 全面負責現有大型企業客戶及潛在客戶的業務。

再次感謝您的時間、考慮，也感謝您費心的面試安排。期待盡快收到您的回音。

楊多莉
敬上

國家圖書館出版品預行編目（CIP）資料

外商‧百大英文面試勝經（MP3 數位下載版）/ 薛詠文
作. -- 初版. -- 臺北市：波斯納出版有限公司, 2022.05
　　面：　公分

　　ISBN 978-626-95821-2-9（平裝）

　　1.CST: 英語　2.CST: 會話　3.CST: 面試

805.188　　　　　　　　　　　　　　　　111004283

外商‧百大英文面試勝經（MP3 數位下載版）
100 Essential Job Interview Questions and Answers

作　　者 / 薛詠文
英文審定 / Quentin Brand
執行編輯 / 莊碧娟

出　　版 / 波斯納出版有限公司
地　　址 / 台北市 100 中正區館前路 26 號 6 樓
電　　話 / (02) 2314-2525
傳　　真 / (02) 2312-3535
郵　　撥 / 19493777 波斯納出版有限公司
客服專線 / (02) 2314-3535
客服信箱 / btservice@betamedia.com.tw

總 經 銷 / 時報文化出版企業股份有限公司
地　　址 / 桃園市龜山區萬壽路二段 351 號
電　　話 / (02) 2306-6842

出版日期 / 2024 年 6 月初版三刷
定　　價 / 360 元
Ｉ Ｓ Ｂ Ｎ / 978-626-95821-2-9

貝塔網址：www.betamedia.com.tw

 喚醒你的英文語感！

Get a Feel for English !